Of Wolves and Men

By

Eileen Sheehan

"When dreams become reality, they can still feel like a dream."

1

"I see two men around you," I said as I pushed my long dark hair back over my shoulders, closed my almond shaped, sapphire blue eyes, and inhaled deeply through my nose. "One is a blue collar worker. He works with chemicals. Tar, I think. I can smell tar. The other is white collar and works around computers in some capacity. The blue collar worker looks to be in his early thirties while the white collar worker looks closer to forty."

The woman sitting opposite of me smiled with satisfaction and eagerly leaned forward as she said, "Yes. That's right! My husband, Jim, works on a road crew. He's thirty-three. The man I'm seeing works in IT. Do you know what that is? It's information technology."

"I'm aware," I informed her with a controlled, bland sounding voice.

It was rare that I turned people away once I agreed to do a psychic reading for them, but I could already tell that I was going to do exactly that with this woman and my mind was whirling as to the correct way to reject her. She struck me as someone who didn't read between the lines, so I'd have to be blunt and direct.

Shrugging her shoulders at my response, the woman's eyes looked starstruck as she continued with, "He's a bit older than me. He's forty-one and I'm twenty-six, but he's so... so..."

"I'm sorry, but I can't read for you," I said as I slid the folded bills that the woman had presented as payment upon sitting down back across the table to her.

"Why?" she asked with dismay. "What's wrong?"

"I had trouble in the past after reading for a woman who was having an affair with a married man," I said with solemnity. "The wife of the husband accused me of supporting the affair. No matter what I said to convince her otherwise, I received the bulk of the blame. She incessantly telephoned both my home and cell phone to harass and threaten me. At one point, she even tried to run my car off the road with her SUV. I was forced to get a restraining order against her." Slowly shaking my head while memories of the ordeal flitted about in my mind, I continued with, "So much negativity. It was annoying, uncomfortable, and a little

4

frightening. I made a promise then and there never to go against my principles and read on situations like that again."

"You don't need to worry about that, George isn't married," she explained with satisfaction.

I instantly knew that was not the truth. What I wasn't sure about was whether she'd been lied to by this man and believed him to be single. With my resolve to stay clear of this mess, I had no intention of going deeper into the subject to find out.

"I'd rather not," I said as I pushed the money even closer toward her.

"But I just found out that I'm pregnant and I need you to tell me who the father of my baby is," she insisted. "It's my first child. I have to know if it's my husband's or George's. I have to know what to do."

I was outraged with the situation. Perhaps I was raised with a moral compass that was outdated, but it infuriated me to think that someone would ask me to use my gifts for something like this. It felt low and degrading. When I was with Rob, he'd have insisted that I do it even if I complained that it made me feel like a circus act. Now that he was out of the picture, I was free to decline.

"There are medical tests for such matters," I said with veiled disgust as I pushed my chair back and stood up.

"Humph," the indignant woman snorted as hands with red nails that looked almost claw-like grabbed her money and haphazardly shoved it into her oversized designer knockoff handbag. Leaping out of her chair with obvious indignation, she snipped, "I've never heard of a psychic with morals."

My blood boiled from the insult, but I managed to remain stoic as I walked to the door and pulled on the doorknob. Holding the thick wooden barrier that separated us from the outside open as wide as I could, I said in a tone that said far more than my facial expression let on, "Please leave."

We were about the same age, but that's where the similarities ended. Samantha Greene was a bottled bleach blonde with a height that made her stand an easy head taller than me. Her large boned structure and appreciation of good food made her easily three times as wide as my slender, petite form, but, at that moment, it was my energy that dominated the space between us.

I pursed my lips as the frustrated woman pushed past me while muttering indignations in such a low level that I didn't bother to try to understand them. Her body language and tone of voice were enough to clue me in to the meaning of the words spewing from collagen infused lips that were painted a brilliant ruby red.

Standing in the doorway, I watched as Samantha aggressively marched to a grey Volkswagen Jetta that was parked along the curb in front of my house. The sound of the car door slamming after she slid behind the driver's wheel was only exceeded by the screeching of tires as the vehicle raced away.

After closing the thick oak exterior door to my circa eighteen hundred home as if it weighed a ton, I leaned against it and sighed. I'd grown weary of the life I'd foolishly created for myself in the small Pennsylvania town that was located on the edge of the Pocono Mountain region.

Having moved there three years earlier after a rough breakup with, Rob, my overbearing fiancé, I'd hoped to find peace and balance within the life of a small town. Instead, I simply attracted more of the same. The only difference was that I was now picking and choosing who I did psychic readings for.

I'd made up my mind to completely stop doing the readings. I'd taken up writing novels and I wanted to only focus on that, but, somehow I'd get talked into doing just one more. It was enough to drive me mad at times. I was furious with myself for not having the where-with-all to say no to these people. I felt like I was trapped on a hamster wheel that wouldn't slow down enough for me to get off. My sanity's saving grace was the friendship I'd developed with the town veterinarian, Kenzie McGovern.

2

Approximately three-thousand people inhabited the village of Freedom. The residents' primary support came from logging and lumber.

Its main street sported an independent grocery store that also housed a pharmacy, a movie theater, two bars, a hardware store, a pizzeria, a Chinese takeout, and a thrift shop. Just around the corner on a small side street was Mildred's Cafe. On the outskirts of town, near the entrance to the highway, was a gas station that had a McDonalds and a Dunkin Donuts inside the store cavity.

Feeling lonely and out of place after unpacking my meager belongings that came nowhere near completing the furnishing of my newly purchased, three-thousand square foot Victorian style home, I'd decided to step out for lunch. I tended to eat light in the midday, so all I wanted was a bowl of soup and a cup of herbal tea. The only place in town to get that was Mildred's Cafe.

Little did I realize when I eagerly made my way to the cozy diner that Mildred's cooking was famed within the area. The tiny establishment offered breakfast and lunch, but was closed for dinner. If residents wanted something to supper on other than what Freedom had to offer, they had to drive twenty miles east to the small city of Wilkes-Barre.

There was exactly one seat left vacant in the crowded café when I entered. It was at the counter. Under normal circumstances, I preferred to sit at a table or a booth. Sitting at the counter made me feel exposed and conspicuous. Since I had no choice if I wanted that bowl of soup -which my stomach was now growling for-, I slid onto the stool and peered at the chalk board where the choices for the soup of the day were neatly written.

"The broccoli cheese is my favorite," said a friendly voice coming from the woman seated to my left. "I'd get that if I were you. It's what I ordered."

The stocky, plain looking woman with short-cropped sandy-blonde hair, no makeup, and clothes that were in typical lumberjack style who was making the suggestion for the soup de jour was Kenzie McGregor. Being the only veterinarian for miles, she was very accustomed to carrying on small talk with people who she barely

10

knew but who knew her or, at least, knew of her, whenever she stepped out.

I found the woman who was my senior by only a few years both entertaining and likable and fell into easy conversation with her. By the time we'd finished our lunch, we'd become fast friends.

Wrestling with animals both big and small provided a semblance of strength in Kenzie that both surprised and impressed me. It was that strength behind the knocking on my door that made it vibrate like someone was trying to beat it down.

"Lisa, are you home?" Kenzie bellowed from the opposite side of the thick barrier. "I only have a few minutes. Open up if you're home, will you?"

Forcing my body to move, I stepped away from the door and swung it opened.

"I have exactly fifteen minutes before I have to get back to the office," Kenzie barked as she marched past me toward the kitchen. "Is there coffee made?" she asked over her shoulder without looking back.

"In the pot, but it's not fresh" I called after her.

I closed the door and made my way to the kitchen in a far less rushed fashion. When I reached it, I found my friend filling a mug with the hours old brew.

Taking a huge gulp of the dark, thickened liquid, she wrinkled her nose and said, "There's no comparison to freshly brewed java, but beggars can't be choosers. It's the caffeine kick that I'm after, anyway."

"Why didn't you stop and get a cup from Mildred's or the gas station?" I asked with curiosity.

"I can't stand that rag water they try to pass off as coffee at the gas station and you know what Mildred's is like at this time of day," Kenzie replied. "I swear, the whole population of Freedom eats out for lunch. I didn't have time to wait in line."

"What's the big hurry?" I asked, with genuine curiosity as I poured out the rest of the old coffee and filled the pot with fresh water to brew a new batch.

"That's why I'm here," she said with excited animation. "An old buddy of mine, Oscar Spears, is in town. We went to veterinary school together. We were quite close for a long time. I'm not sure why, but we lost touch over the last year."

I knit my brows together in thought. "I think you've mentioned him."

She nodded.

"I'm sure I have," she said as she pulled the carafe out from the steam of freshly brewed coffee and held her now empty mug beneath it until it was half-full. Placing the carafe back in its rightful place, she splashed a bit of cream into her rich, dark brew and sniffed it appreciatively. "He's meeting me for dinner to discuss some sort of proposition that he has."

"Romance or business?" I asked.

Kenzie vigorously shook her head as she admitted that there had never been romance between them.

"He's very good looking," she said with a hefty sigh, "but we just never took it past friendship. Not that I would have minded, mind you…"

"Maybe he's ready," I wistfully mused.

She threw her head back in laughter.

Her fondness for me was apparent as she good naturedly said, "For someone who is anti-relationship, you seem pretty hell bent on pairing me up with this guy."

I scowled at the remark. I didn't like to think of myself as being anti-relationship. Yet, in many ways I was still recovering from my breakup so I wasn't in a rush to get involved again. I could see where that could be construed as anti-relationship, but I didn't like it.

"It's not that," I explained. "It's just that I sometimes get lonely so I figure you do too. Having a man on occasion to fill in that loneliness might be nice."

"Are you telling me that you're ready to jump back onto the dating train?" she asked with surprise.

"Not yet," I replied, "but that doesn't mean that you need to stay alone."

"I'm not alone," Kenzie informed her. "I just don't talk about my private business.

I gave a mockingly innocent smile, "Not even to me?"

"Especially not to you, you mind reading witch," my friend teased back.

Our light-hearted bantering brought back thoughts of my last client and I sighed.

"Did I offend you?" she apologetically asked. "I'm sorry. It was a joke."

I gave a slight shake of my head. Even though I didn't do the psychic reading for Samantha Greene, I still withheld her name as I proceeded to explain what had occurred just minutes before Kenzie had arrived. Knowing how strongly I felt about client confidentiality, she never asked for the identity of the cheating married woman who had no idea who the father of her baby was.

"I thought you said that you were stopping the readings for people," Kenzie said with a scowl. "Isn't that one of the things you wanted to leave behind when you moved here? I mean, it's not like you need the money or anything. Your inheritance is enough to last beyond your years on this earth if you stay in this little town. Plus, you get your book royalties. Why bother with readings?"

"This was a special request from Cali, a friend from back home. The woman traveled ninety minutes to see me. She shouldn't have wasted her time," I said. "The shame is on me. I should have checked to see what the reading would be about when I was scheduling her. I usually do, but I thought Cali knew better."

"Perhaps this Cali didn't think to find out what the woman wanted before asking you to do the favor. Anyway, I don't know how you are able to know things about people like that," Kenzie said. "I know it's becoming more and more acceptable with society, but it kind of freaks me out."

"It did me for years," I admitted. "It was Rob who finally got me to be comfortable with my abilities and who taught me how to use them correctly. I never enjoyed it, though. I did it mainly to appease him. After breaking up with him, I wanted nothing more to do with it. Unfortunately, things like that have a tendency to follow a person. Once a psychic, always a psychic, I guess."

"Not if you don't want it," Kenzie said with a smile.

"I don't, but then, there are times when I do," I mused. "I think I'd like to only use my abilities if and when I feel like it instead of on demand by strangers."

Setting down her coffee mug, Kenzie headed for the door. "That's completely understandable. I have to run, but I thought you'd like to meet Oscar. Join us for dinner tonight?"

"Where?" I asked.

With a sheepish grin, Kenzie said, "How about your back patio? I'll bring takeout."

After a roll of my eyes, a friendly, knowing smile, a slow shake of my head, and a slight sigh of resignation, I nodded in agreement.

"It will be late," Kenzie said. "I have surgery this afternoon. Shall we say eight?"

"Let me guess," I chuckled. "Chinese or pizza."

"I thought Chinese," she good naturedly replied as she raced out of the house toward her car.

3

If I considered myself a quiet people watcher who struggled to find small talk in a room full of strangers, it was never more so than during that dinner at my patio table beneath the brilliancy of the starry night. There may have only been one stranger amidst the trio, but his presence was so overwhelming that it felt almost crowded.

Oscar Spears was a handsome, dark haired man with piercing dark eyes that I swore looked right into my soul. His six-foot, three-inch physique was lean and muscular beneath a form fitting tee shirt and denim jeans. When he stood next to me, I felt small and almost fragile. Even though I was petite and shorter than most of the people I encountered, it was a feeling that I wasn't exactly comfortable with. Therefore, I kept my distance.

Kenzie was five-feet-seven, which was an easy four inches taller than me. Her bone and muscle structure made her appear much larger and bulkier than she was when we stood beside each other. Even so, I didn't feel inferior to the woman like I did with Oscar.

We'd eaten most of our meal with the conversation flowing between my friend and the handsome veterinarian; their main topic being their work. Since I found it to be an interesting subject, I was content to sit and listen.

"We're boring you with our shop talk," Oscar finally said in a rich, deep vibrato.

"Not at all," I said with a touch of nervousness.

I couldn't explain what it was about this man that set me off balance. It wasn't my style to allow men... any man... to do that to me. I liked men, true, but I wasn't desperate to have one in my life like many of the women I'd met.

That was one of the things about Kenzie that I enjoyed. She didn't display man craving tendencies. When we got together, we discussed interesting topics instead of the catty or needy conversations about men and female competition that I'd endured in so many female gatherings.

"Lisa is a typical writer," Kenzie teasingly offered. "She's a quiet people watcher."

Oscar raised a brow.

"Is that so?" he said with a tone that showed that he was impressed. "What do you write?"

"Nothing epic," I eagerly offered. "It's mainly genre stuff."

"Such as...," he continued.

"I enjoy writing romance thrillers," I replied.

"Paranormal romance thrillers," Kenzie added.

Oscar grinned and studied me with a bit more care than I was comfortable with.

"Do you believe in the paranormal?" he asked.

I shrugged. "I believe in ghosts and such."

He had a hint of sincerity in his voice as he asked, "Just ghosts?"

"She has some kind of psychic ability," Kenzie offered. When I shot her a look of disapproval, she quickly added, "But, she doesn't like to talk about it or use it."

"Why not?" he asked with surprise.

The disappointment that I felt at his question was almost overwhelming. This man was the first man in three years that came anywhere close to being someone who I found attractive and interesting enough to grab my attention. I didn't know if it was the way he'd asked it or simply the question, but instead of being relieved that he wouldn't look at me as a freak, it saddened me. I was instantly reminded of Rob, who I'd allowed to exploit my psychic gifts for his own personal gain for far too many years. Without realizing it, Oscar had placed himself in that same category with those two simple words.

Whether it was my facial expression and body language or that my sudden mood change seemed to spread throughout the patio, I could see recognition that he'd said something wrong in Oscar.

He validated it when he worriedly apologized for upsetting me.

Before I could respond to his apology, Kenzie quickly interjected with more inappropriate divulging of my private business by saying, "Lisa's ex-fiancé tried to turn her into a circus act."

I had opened my mouth to say something, but not that. Snapping it shut, I shot my friend a look of warning that hit home.

Quickly interpreting the meaning of my stern look, Kenzie good naturedly said, "Maybe we should change the subject to something less personal."

Oscar's eyes remained stoic while his mouth formed a friendly smile.

Turning to Kenzie, he said, "So, then, let's talk about why I'm here."

Kenzie chuckled, "I thought it was for our fair company."

"True," he good naturedly replied, "but there's also a motive behind my visit. Are you up for a challenge?"

With a look of surprised excitement, she replied, "It depends. Is it dangerous?"

"It can be," he said with a grin. "I've been commissioned to tag a few wolves for part of a study of the wildlife in the Appalachian mountains. There's a lot of ground to cover with time restrictions. I could use some help."

"You want me to walk away from my practice to tag wildlife?" she asked with disbelief.

"Wolves, actually," he corrected her. "To tag wolves." After a brief silence, he added, "I don't expect you to walk away. Just give me a few days of your help. When was the last time you took a vacation? Look at it as a vacation from the mundane of everyday vet work."

"A vacation would be somewhere on the beach with a drink that sports a tiny umbrella in my hand," she replied.

"Where's your spirit of adventure?" he asked. Then, with sincerity, he added, "My guy who was supposed to help broke his leg. I'm in a bind here, Kenz."

"Where?" she briskly asked.

"That's just it," he said. "I have to cover the Poconos and a piece of downstate New York. I thought I'd put you in the Poconos since my family has a cabin there and then I'll take New York."

"No tent?" she jokingly asked.

"The tent will go with me," he smugly stated. "You, on the other hand, get to live in the lap of luxury."

"I think I remember you mentioning that cabin, but I don't recall you describing it as luxurious," she said with humor. Then, with a bit more seriousness, she asked, "It's pretty remote, isn't it?"

He nodded as he said with an obvious sense of pride, "Very. It's almost heaven, but still fairly close to civilization if you need it."

"The best of both worlds," I interjected.

Oscar and Kenzie looked at me as if they were just then remembering that I was in their company.

"Can I take Lisa with me?" she asked.

"What?" I blurted out. "I know nothing about tagging wolves."

"It would be a nice place for you to find that quiet you've been craving," Kenzie explained. "You might even get that book done. You can write during the day while I'm out tagging and then, in the evenings, we can enjoy the great outdoors with a glass of wine or something."

I looked at Oscar and said in a low voice, "I could stand to get away for a while."

He gave a broad, sincere smile and said, "Mi casa su casa."

I briefly studied him while I tried to inconspicuously determine what it was about him that made my insides flutter, and not necessarily in a good way. I was getting an intuitive warning, but for the life of me, I couldn't grasp the reason behind it. Oscar was a handsome, well-groomed, educated man who was clearly well liked by Kenzie and I trusted Kenzie.

Brushing the feeling off as simple remnants from my associating him with Rob, I smiled and said, "Thank you."

"It's settled, then," Kenzie said as she refilled our wine glasses. "So, tell me about this job. When do we leave and how long do we have to complete it? I'll need to notify my patients and figure out what to do in the case of an emergency."

A sense of both relief and excitement swept through me as I quietly sipped my wine while listening to Kenzie and Oscar discuss the job and plan it out as best as they could. Getting away into the mountains was just the thing that I needed to clear my head and regain my sanity and, like Kenzie suggested, write my novel.

4

"There's no bathroom," I moaned with dismay as I stepped out onto the front porch after inspecting the inside of the cabin.

"There's an outhouse," Kenzie offered as she climbed the small set of steps that separated the porch from the dirt patch where she'd parked the SUV. "There's electricity and running water, though."

"The lap of luxury, eh?" I chided with a mixture of amusement and irritation.

Kenzie gave me a look of chagrin, "I guess I neglected to ask about a bathroom. It's a good lesson in never assuming." Heaving a sigh, she added, "The weather's lovely and we have that huge lake just up the road. It looked like a healthy body of water. We can bathe there and, like I said, there's an outhouse."

"It's fine," I assured her. "I was just a little taken aback, that's all."

"Some people's idea of heaven doesn't match up with ours," she chuckled.

"Ideally, heaven would have a toilet

and a shower, but, if I recall, he said it was *almost* heaven," I joked, with an emphasis on the word, almost.

"Oh, well. If he said almost, then he's in the clear," she noted as she picked up her bag and headed inside. "Tell me that we at least have our own rooms."

"I took the one in the back since I didn't know what ungodly hour you might decide to head out to do this tagging stuff," I informed her.

"Smart," she said over her shoulder as she disappeared through the doorway of the closest of the two bedrooms. After quickly depositing her bags just inside the door, she returned to the main room that consisted of the kitchen, dining area, and living room and took a good look around. "It's pretty rustic."

"I like it," I admitted. "Step outside and take a minute to really look around and you'll understand Oscar's claim. This place is fabulous."

We walked out onto the porch and took in our surroundings with eyes and minds that were no longer concerned about bathrooms, showers, or where we were going to sleep.

Our expressions reflected the awe and appreciation that we were experiencing for the beauty of nature that enveloped us.

The cabin was at the end of a mile long dirt drive that wound its way up the side of a mountain until it reached a clearing. There, in the middle of the clearing, was the small, two bedroom, one-hundred year old log cabin.

Noting how deep into the woods that the cabin was, I made mention of how impressive it was that Oscar's family was able to get the electric company to run electricity to it. It was then that Kenzie admitted that the electricity was provided by a gas generator that was located behind the cabin and needed to be started.

Instead of dulling my appreciation for the place, it actually increased it. I'd spent years fantasizing about staying in a place like this with the bare necessities at my disposal, but I'd never had the opportunity present itself. Before moving to Freedom, I'd associated with a circle of friends whose idea of roughing it was going downstairs in the hotel for a continental breakfast and I'd not had the guts or the drive to initiate such a stay on my own.

With the late afternoon sun behind her, a slight glow that resembled a halo framed Kenzie's head as I looked at her and said, "Thank you."

Surprised, my good friend asked, "For what?"

I spread my arms wide and enthusiastically said, "This. Thank you for this."

She chuckled. "Don't mention it. Now, what do you think? Should we get that generator running and unpack the food?"

"I have absolutely no clue how to operate that generator," I confessed.

"I didn't think you would, miss fancy pants," Kenzie said with humor. "Lucky for us that I'm part tomboy. I know my way around a generator, a hatchet, and a campfire."

"Praise be," I mockingly bellowed.

"Ha," Kenzie said as she placed her hands on her hips. With a curt smile, she said, "Just you stick with me, kiddo. I'll make a tomboy out of you yet."

I rolled my eyes as I placed my hand over my chest and said, "Be still my heart. I can hardly wait."

After taking a moment to enjoy the humor, Kenzie headed for the generator while I proceeded to unpack the food and supplies that we'd brought. When I came upon the wine, I opened a bottle to let it breathe for the length of time it would take her to return from setting the cabin aright with electricity.

The sound of a vehicle coming up the long dirt drive reached my ears long before Oscar's jeep could be seen through the thick foliage covered landscape. Kenzie was just coming around to the front of the cabin after successfully mastering the generator when I joined her on the front porch to greet our host.

Parking his jeep next to our SUV, Oscar lept out of the vehicle wearing a smile and an outfit that shouted camouflage. From his hat to his jacket and his pants, he blended with his surroundings to the point where I doubted I'd be able to spot him if he left the clearing.

"Wow!" Kenzie said with enthusiastic delight. "That's some getup."

"Don't be jealous," he teased, "There's one for you in my jeep."

"Seriously?" she squealed with mocking delight. "I've always wanted to dress like the forest."

"Tease all you want," he replied. "You'll thank me after a day or two of tracking."

Kenzie's face grew somber as she asked, "Is it that difficult?"

He shrugged as he said, "It can be, but being invisible helps."

"What about your scent," I asked. "Even being invisible won't help if they smell you."

Both surprised and impressed by my insight, Oscar turned to me and said, "That's a good question. We have a special perfume to wear."

"Eau de wolf, I assume," Kenzie said with a sarcastic sigh.

"Wolf what?" I suspiciously asked as all kinds of crazy thoughts flitted through my mind as to how they'd produce a wolf scent. I hoped it didn't involve blood or the like. It was at that moment that I realized that I was associating blood with Oscar. Of course, I quickly rationalized it by remembering that he was a veterinarian. "Where do you get wolf scent?"

"It comes from their scent glands," Kenzie explained. "It's like their personal calling card."

"Yes," Oscar nodded, "It helps, but also can be dangerous because it's not only how they identify a wolf, but it's how they can tell if you're part of their pack or part of a rival pack."

"What happens if it's a rival pack?" I asked while thinking that I probably already knew the answer.

"It can get hairy," Oscar replied.

"Speaking of packs," I continued. "Don't they travel in packs?"

"They do," Kenzie offered.

"How do you plan on tagging a pack?" I asked with concern. "You're just one person."

"There are what we call lone wolves," Oscar explained. "They're low on the totem pole and will sometimes be so mistreated that they leave the pack and go it alone. They're who we're wanting to study. We want to see if they remain alone or if they eventually find a new pack."

"That doesn't sound easy," I observed.

"That's why they're paying us the big bucks," Kenzie chuckled.

"Oh," I said with a hint of surprise. "I actually forgot that you were being paid for this. It's so nice out here that I forgot that we're technically here on business."

Oscar moved closer to me as he said, "So, you like my little piece of heaven?"

"I'd like it more if it had a toilet and a shower," I chided, "but it's beautiful beyond description."

"We have an outhouse and the lake over there is fresh and ready for bathing," he said with enthusiasm.

"That's what I said," Kenzie interjected.

I looked from Kenzie to Oscar and then back again. They really were birds of a feather. I thought about the type of couple they'd make and decided that they were well suited for dating. Not only that, but it was clear that they had extremely fond feelings for each other. What I couldn't understand was why neither of them made an effort to take it beyond friendship.

5

"I want to thank you for having the foresight to get the place cleaned for us," Kenzie said as she put the last of the perishables into the refrigerator and closed the door.

"Yes," I added, "I thought we'd be spending our first few hours getting it livable. It was a pleasant surprise to see it so neat and clean."

"I'd like to take the credit," Oscar admitted as he sat down in one of the overstuffed chairs in the living room section of the great room and accepted the wine glass that Kenzie offered him, "but it wasn't my doing. Noah uses this cabin a lot. He never knows when he'll be able to come or if he'll arrive in the day or the night so he has a cleaner from the nearby town come in biweekly to make sure it's all up to snuff. The man hates dust."

"That explains why I didn't need to prime the generator to get it going," Kenzie mused.

"Yes, it would," Oscar agreed.

"Does Noah live nearby?" I asked with genuine curiosity.

"His house isn't that far from here," Oscar replied, "but he travels a wide area for work so he doesn't have a schedule like most would for using the place."

"He's a wildlife trooper, isn't he?" Kenzie asked.

"He's actually a game warden," Oscar corrected her, "but he sometimes doubles as a trooper during the heavy tourist season."

The sound of tires grinding up the winding mountainside dirt road caught our attention.

"Speak of the devil. I'll wager that's him," Oscar enthusiastically said as he stood up.

He carefully set his wine glass on a nearby table before briskly walking out of the cabin to watch the vehicle's arrival from the front porch.

Kenzie was quick to follow her friend, but I lagged back. That feeling of nervous dread that I'd experienced when I'd first met Oscar had come back at an alarming intensity.

I went to the kitchen and freshened my glass of wine. Leaning against the counter, I slowly sipped my pinot noir while listening to Oscar introduce Kenzie to his brother.

Noah's voice was similar to Oscar's with its deep richness as he said, "I thought you said that there would be two staying in the cabin."

I suddenly felt very foolish about hiding in the kitchen. I was in the process of frantically trying to figure out what to do or say to explain why I hadn't gone out onto the porch to greet him along with Kenzie and Oscar when the trio wandered into the cabin.

"Kenzie said that you were a quiet people watcher, not that you were also shy," Oscar light-heartedly said as he sauntered up to the counter with a type of regal confidence that was impossible to ignore.

I gave a slight shrug and emitted an uncomfortable giggle as I looked past Oscar at his brother. As if on cue, my body instantly reacted to the pheromones that his brother was emitting. My legs literally buckled beneath me. I did my best to inconspicuously grab hold of the counter to prevent myself from falling while praying that no one noticed what was happening.

No such luck.

"Are you alright?" Noah asked as he moved with impressive speed to place his hands on my waist in an effort to set me aright.

The feel of his strong, extremely warm hands sent shivers of delight through my body from head to toe. I inhaled his musky scent as if he was wearing Roja perfume for men. It took me a moment to find the courage to look into his deep-set dark eyes. When I did, they had the same effect, if not more so, as Oscar's had. They bore into my inner core and held me firmly in place. His dark hair was cut short and allowed to lay as it pleased in a way that made it obvious that he was a man who was either clueless of how handsome he was or simply didn't care.

Noah placed his face so close to the side of my head that the heat of his breath caressed my flesh. His words reverberated in my ear canal as he said in a low voice that I doubted Oscar or Kenzie heard, "You're trembling."

"I...I'm okay," I stammered in a hoarse whisper that surprised me. "I think I just need to eat something. I'm feeling a little light- headed."

"If that's the case, is wine a wise choice of drink?" he asked in a way that made me feel like a foolish child.

Suddenly annoyed with this hot and sexy guy who had the audacity to judge me, I indignantly pulled from his hold.

"There's no need to worry about me," I snapped in a low tone that was meant for his ears only.

"Okay, then," he said with mild amusement. "I won't."

He turned his attention back to his brother and Kenzie without giving me a second glance. To my annoyance, his dismissive behavior only served to infuriate me more.

After a few minutes of conversation with my friend and his brother, Noah excused himself as he asked to speak with Oscar alone.

With the men no longer monopolizing her attention, Kenzie turned to me.

"So, what do you think of the brother?" she asked. "It's my first time meeting Noah. Oscar spoke of him often, but he didn't do him justice. He's pretty hot, don't you think? I mean, Oscar is good looking enough, but there's something about Noah. It's an underlying thing. Exciting. Maybe even mysterious. You know?"

I simply gave a slight nod while I stayed planted where Noah had left me in the kitchen. I still didn't trust my legs. To add to that worry, I had to hope that my astute friend didn't realize how utterly thrown off and annoyed I was from my little encounter with the handsome and sexy brother of her equally handsome and sexy friend.

6

The brothers had walked off into the woods to have their conversation. Since I hadn't watched them leave, I had no idea of the direction they'd taken.

"I need to use our trusty outhouse," I said when my legs finally felt usable again. Heading out to the porch, I surveyed the clearing before asking, "Do you happen to know where it's located.

"I'm assuming it's hidden behind the building," Kenzie offered. "I didn't see it when I was starting the generator, but I wasn't looking for it. My guess is it's back there."

"It's a bit odd to hide an outhouse, isn't it?" I asked with mild annoyance.

"Do you really want a shithouse sitting in plain view of the cabin?" Kenzie asked with amusement. "Not to mention what happens when the wind kicks up."

"Egad," I said with a roll of my eyes as I stepped off the porch and headed toward the back side of the cabin. "What did I get myself into?"

"There's my city girl," Kenzie teased. "Do we need to mark the trees so that you can find your way back?"

"Very funny," I called over my shoulder as I left the clearing to search for the outhouse amidst the trees that bordered it. "Just finish unpacking and setting up, will you? I'm getting hungry."

"Unpack and set up?" Kenzie exclaimed. "How long do you plan on being?"

Her unbridled laughter floated back to me as I continued to walk while flipping my middle finger without looking back at her.

My bladder was about to burst and I saw no signs of the outhouse. If I didn't find it soon, I'd have no choice but to go where I stood.

Not only was there no outhouse in sight, but I was feeling a touch of trepidation over the distance that was building between me and the cabin. I'd been so preoccupied with thoughts of Noah and the unsettling effect that he'd had on me that I'd paid little attention to my surroundings. Kenzie wasn't far off with her suggestion to mark the path that I'd taken. It might have proven useful.

Studying my surroundings for the first time, I realized that I'd gone much further into the wild than I'd intended and wasn't altogether sure of the direction I'd walked in.

The adrenaline that coursed through my veins as my mind whirled with scenes from all of the horror shows I'd watched over the years where monsters or predatory wildlife hunted humans in the woods and did unspeakable things to them, including eating them, caused my bladder to threaten to give way on its own if I didn't immediately empty it. Seeing no alternative, I dropped my pants to my ankles and squatted where I stood.

The silence of the forest was assaulted by the seemingly amplified sound of the almost endless stream of my urine beating against the debris on the forest floor. A sense of uneasiness came over me to the extent that I felt panicked. I mentally begged my bladder to finish relieving itself quickly so that I could hurry back to the cabin.

I was just fastening my pants when a low snarl caught my attention. Almost frozen with fear, I slowly looked to my right. There, just a few yards away, stood an enormous snow white wolf. Had I not been so terrified, I'd have delighted in admiring its thick, beautiful coat. Unfortunately, my eyes were locked on the long, solid looking fangs that it displayed.

I squeezed my eyes shut while I thought on what to do. Running would be foolish since the wolf was close and much faster than I was. Could I use my psychic abilities to speak to it telepathically? I'd done it a few times with domestic dogs and cats. Even if I could, would it do me any good to tell it that I meant it no harm? It was a wild creature and a predator, after all.

My heartbeat was so strong that it pounded against my eardrums, making it difficult to hear much else. It was for this reason that I didn't hear Noah approaching.

"What are you doing?" he asked with a hint of agitation. "Did you just urinate?"

I opened my eyes with a start to find Noah standing with his hand on the back of the beautiful, yet super scary wolf and a look of annoyance on his face.

"We have an outhouse for a reason," he continued. "Your urine is going to attract the wolves in the area, or worse."

"I was looking for it," I feebly explained while not taking my eyes off the wolf.

His face softened a bit as he said, "You're not an outdoors kind of person, are you?" When I vigorously shook my head, he asked, "Can I ask why you came up here with Kenzie?"

Seeing that the wolf was content to stand next to Noah and have its ears scratched, I allowed my body to relax enough to converse with him.

"I needed to get away and Kenzie thought this was the perfect opportunity," I explained. "I'm not a total idiot when it comes to the wild. I've just never had the opportunity to enjoy it like this. It's all new. That's all."

"I see," he said as his mesmerizing eyes studied me. After an uncomfortable silence that felt like hours, but I guessed were only seconds, he added, "This is Snow. He lives in these parts. Since you've ventured into his territory and he's now aware of you, you might as well get acquainted."

As he moved toward me, the wolf did the same. With a renewed panic, I quickly stepped back.

"Stand still and let him smell you," Noah practically barked. "This can go good or bad. The choice is yours."

"If I let him smell me, will it go good?" I meekly asked.

He nodded and said in a low tone, "That's what I'm hoping for."

Snow's moist nose felt cold as it brushed against the back of my trembling hand.

"You're hoping?" I said with obvious distress.

"Just stay as calm as you can and let him sniff you," Noah ordered.

After what had to be the most torturous few minutes of my life, the wolf completed its sniffing of my entire body. I doubted it left one inch out. When it finally walked back to Noah, I heaved a sigh of relief.

The fear that had kept me standing like a statue gushed from me like the waters that were held back by a dam that suddenly broke. The result was my legs failing me and the world going black.

The sound of a wolf howling was the last thing I heard before I slipped into oblivion.

7

The male voices sounded distant as I slowly regained consciousness. It took my head a moment to clear enough for me to realize that I was being carried by one of them and he wasn't being particularly cautious about jostling me about.

Confused and uncertain of what to do, I kept my eyes closed while I focused on the words being passed back and forth between the two brothers.

"I can't believe you brought them here just before the full moon. What were you thinking?" snapped Noah.

"I had no choice," Oscar defensively said. "I'm on a time crunch. Kenzie's the only one I could find to help at the last minute. When she asked to bring Lisa, what was I supposed to say... no psychics allowed?"

"It's bad enough that she's psychic and could pick up on something, but she carries a touch of the bloodline," Noah complained. "It's faint, but I could smell it in her urine. We'll be lucky if they leave her alone now that she's marked the woods with her piss."

"Yes," Oscar mused. "That's unfortunate."

"It would have been so simple to give them a small tour of the place upon arrival," Noah criticized.

"I got here only minutes before you did, brother," Oscar barked.

I could feel Noah's chest fill with air and then purge it out in a sigh of resignation.

"Well," he huffed, "I can't babysit her the entire time. I'll have to leave Snow here."

"Is he enough?" Oscar hesitantly asked.

"He'll do what he's told," Noah replied.

"But is he enough," Oscar asked again.

"It depends on who comes and how many," Noah replied. "Does Kenzie know anything?"

"No," Oscar said in earnest. "To tell you the truth, I had it in my head that they'd bypass this place and we wouldn't have to say anything."

"Not with that pool of urine she left behind. The woman's got one hell of a bladder to hold that much," Noah grumbled. "We'll be lucky if half the mountain doesn't pick up on it."

"Can we disguise the scent?" Oscar hopefully asked. "We have a few days before the moon is full."

"I plan on covering it as much as possible, but it's soaked into the ground," Noah said. "Maybe, if we're lucky, we can mask it at least enough that it doesn't draw those from the other side of the mountain."

"We should still probably tell Kenzie," Oscar suggested.

"Is she trustworthy?" Noah asked with concern.

"I mean to marry her one day," Oscar replied.

"Don't you think you should date her first?" Noah asked with a chuckle.

"There is that," Oscar chuckled back.

"Damn, what a mess," Noah huffed.

Unable to keep quiet any longer, I opened my eyes and looked at the strong jaw of the man who held me in his arms.

We were almost to the cabin when I said, "People pee in the wild all the time. I don't know why my doing it is such a big deal."

"It's not the pee, but who did the peeing," Oscar mysteriously said.

Looking at him as if he had four heads, I scowled as I complained that I had no clue what he was talking about.

"It's you," Noah offered. "You've got specific genetics that leave a special scent.

It's unlike that of the normal human."

"I'm a normal human," I protested.

"The hell you are," Oscar blurted out.

Feeling alert and agitated, I looked into Noah's dark, bottomless eyes and said in a firm voice, "You can put me down now. I can walk."

His eyes lit up with what I assumed was amusement as he said, "I have no doubt that you can."

To my surprise, he made no move to put me down. Instead, he climbed the steps to the porch with such ease and grace that one would have thought that he was carrying a pillow instead of a one-hundred-ten-pound female.

Oscar scooted ahead and opened the door to the cabin so that his brother could continue without interruption. It wasn't until we were well into the room before Noah unceremoniously dropped me onto the sofa.

"What's going on?" Kenzie asked as she scurried to check on me.

Her look of concern shifted to amusement once she realized that I was perfectly fine and simply fuming inside over Noah's behavior. She could feel the chemistry between him and me, but could also feel us both resisting it. If Noah stuck around, she bet it would prove interesting to see how things progressed.

Before anyone could explain the dynamics of the situation, Snow appeared in the doorway. Kenzie sucked in her breath, but made no other noise as she stared, wide-eyed, at the beautiful beast.

Seeing her reaction, Oscar slapped the side of his thigh and called the wolf to him. Snow obediently moved next to the handsome veterinarian like a dog might a master.

Scratching the beast behind its ears, Oscar lightheartedly said, "Meet Snow."

"He's beautiful," Kenzie muttered with awe.

"He's going to be staying with you while you're here," Noah offered.

"The hell he is," I blurted out.

Snow snarled and Oscar raised a brow.

"I was under the impression that you two made friends," he said.

"If you mean my standing still, terrified, while it sniffed me from head to toe is making friends, then, I guess we did," I said, "but it was one sided."

"How so?" Noah asked.

"I never sniffed back," I announced.

Whether it was meant to be funny or not, my remark got a roar of laughter from the room until I eventually joined in.

"Have you any idea how scary that

was?" I asked when the laughter settled down.

"Lisa's an author and a city girl," Kenzie explained. "She's not used to being around domestic animals, let alone wild ones."

"So, she came into the deep woods where there are wild animals all about to relax?" Noah incredulously pointed out.

"Piss off," I snapped.

I'd had just about as much of his pompous attitude as I could stand. Host or no host, the man was rude and insulting.

"I'd say you did enough of that for all of us," Noah chuckled.

"You do have one king sized bladder," Oscar noted.

"Are we back on this topic again?" I asked with exasperation.

"What topic?' Kenzie asked with confusion. "Your bladder?"

"I couldn't find the outhouse, so I peed in the woods," I explained. "Apparently, that's a no-no."

"Peeing in the woods is a no-no?" Kenzie repeated with confusion. "Someone needs to explain what's going on. I'm very confused."

Oscar eyed Noah as he said, "We have something to discuss. You might want to sit down for it."

8

After directing Snow to settle in front of the fireplace at the far end of the great room and making sure that everyone was seated in a comfortable position in preparation for the talk, Noah was the first to break into conversation.

Focusing his attention on Kenzie he said, "I'm aware that you and my brother go back some years." When she nodded, he continued, "He thinks very highly of you which is why we're trusting you with something that's been held secret."

"Not just from you, Kenz. From everyone," Oscar quickly interjected.

"I see," Kenzie said in a slow and thoughtful manner. "Is this a secret that I want to know or should even know?"

"I'm not sure you'll want to know it, but you definitely need to know it," Oscar replied.

Kenzie looked at me and said, "What about Lisa? I'm assuming she needs to hear this secret too?"

Noah slowly nodded as he said in a low tone, "She's left us no options."

"What?" I gasped. "How? By peeing in the woods?"

"Exactly," Noah replied.

Kenzie massaged her temples with her fingertips as she mumbled, "I'm so confused."

"Let my brother speak and soon it will all be clear," Oscar said with compassion.

She gave me a pleading look before turning to Noah and saying, "Go ahead."

Filling his lungs with air as if to fortify himself for what he was about to say, Noah slowly released it along with the following words, "There are things that are spoken in fairy tales that are, in truth, something very real. Since Lisa is psychic, I'm guessing that she'll be easier to convince about this fact than you, Kenzie."

"Don't be so quick to judge," Kenzie blurted out. "I believe in things that go bump in the night."

"Like ghosts, right?" Oscar enthusiastically asked.

"Sure," Kenzie said with a nod. "Ghosts are real."

"What about vampires and werewolves?" Noah asked.

Kenzie looked at me. I simply raised a brow and, in mocking silence, mouthed the words *vampires* and *werewolves*.

"Either one," Oscar said with encouragement.

"Well," Kenzie mused. "I believe that there is a basis for these fairy tales even though they may not be exactly as they are described in the stories."

Noah turned to me and asked, "And you? What about you? Do you believe in vampires and werewolves?"

"Nope," I said with a flat tone.

"Seriously?" Oscar exclaimed. "But you're psychic."

"One has nothing to do with the other," I calmly protested.

Noah gave a sarcastic chuckle. "So, the vet believes in werewolves and the psychic doesn't. Now, that's a twist I wasn't prepared for."

I leaned forward and looked directly at him as I said, "I believe in things that I see, hear, or touch. I've seen and spoken to ghosts. I've never seen or heard a vampire or a werewolf."

"Yes, you have," Oscar insisted. "At least a werewolf, you have."

Kenzie looked aghast as she said, "What are you talking about, Oscar? Are you trying to tell us that Snow is a werewolf?"

Noah cleared his throat loud enough to grab the room's attention. "What he's trying to tell you is that he and I come from a lineage of unique humans who turn canine upon the full moon."

"Canine?" Kenzie repeated with confusion.

"Like a werewolf?" I said with disbelief.

"Not like a werewolf," Noah replied, "but a werewolf."

I hopped to my feet and snarled, "Stop this right now. I don't know what you're up to, but this isn't funny."

Feeling the tension in the air, Snow stood up and snarled in my direction.

"Sit down, please," Noah said in a calm voice before turning to Snow and firmly saying, "Down boy."

I turned to Kenzie and said, "I think I should just go home."

"You can't," Noah and Oscar simultaneously bellowed.

"What?" Kenzie asked while I blurted out, "Why not?"

Noah took another deep breath before pouring out the words, "Because you're one of us. Not full blooded and born like us, but you carry the gene that will allow them to turn you into one of us."

"What nonsense..." I began.

"It's not nonsense," Oscar insisted. "It's true and, now that you've made it known that you're here by leaving your scent in the woods, there are those who will want to add you to their pack. We're a dwindling breed. Adding a fertile female to the pack is

51

a desirable thing."

"I'm going home," I said as I stood up once more.

"They'll follow you there," Noah warned. "If they get into town, there's no telling what havoc will occur or how many lives will be lost as they search for you. It's best that you stay here and let us protect you."

"We're going to cover the ground where you left your scent with our own and hope that it's enough to keep them away," Oscar said. "We'll know soon enough. The full moon is upon us."

Kenzie was the one to stand up and pace this time. "Let me get this straight," she mused aloud. "What you're telling me is that my best buddy from college is a werewolf and that my bestie girlfriend is not just a psychic, but a werewolf as well?"

"Not a werewolf, exactly," Noah informed her. "She just carries the genes that will allow her to be turned into a werewolf. You see, not everyone who is attacked by a werewolf becomes one. You have to have the right genetics. Those who don't simply die."

"Always?" Kenzie asked with concern.

"Not always," Oscar said. "Sometimes they recover. That's why the world knows about werewolves."

"Because the people who recover tell

about the attack," I thoughtfully said.

"And the world doesn't believe them," Kenzie added.

Standing up and clapping his hands with approval, Oscar said, "Exactly."

"Wow," Kenzie mumbled as she slumped against the sofa's back cushion.

"I know it's a shocker, Kenz," Oscar apologetically said. "I didn't want to have to tell you this way. I was going to eventually share our secret with you because I... uh... well, I was hoping to take our relationship further, but this isn't how I wanted you to find out."

"Further?" Kenzie wistfully said in a daze-like manner.

"Are you okay, Kenzie?" Noah asked with concern.

She nodded while never taking her eyes off Oscar. She was not only processing the fact that he was a werewolf, but that he'd finally decided to take their relationship to another level. The issue at hand was whether or not she wanted to do the same, now that she knew that he was a werewolf.

"So, I'm stuck here while I wait to see if they'll come for me," I moaned while ignoring the dynamics between Oscar and my friend. "This is a nightmare."

"I'm leaving Snow with you," Noah offered.

"Why?" I asked as I looked at the scary beast and shuttered. "You said we have time before the full moon."

"There might be a straggler about," he replied. "If so, it's too late to cover your scent and he just might try to capture you prior to the full moon to assure you don't get taken by another pack."

Noah's stern look suddenly turned to concern and compassion as he watched a lone tear slide down my cheek.

"I'm so sorry," he said with what sounded like genuine remorse.

"Yes," Oscar added. "I never would have had you come if I'd known what you were. I just thought you were a psychic who wrote books."

"That's what I am," I pouted. "It's all I want to be. In fact, I don't even want to be a psychic. I just want to write books and enjoy life."

"Then, we'll do our best to make sure things stay that way," Noah said with conviction. "Oscar and Kenzie will focus on finding and tagging the lone wolves with record speed and I'll try to stop by while they're gone to check on you. Snow will be your constant companion."

I looked at Snow and shuddered.

"Give him a chance," Kenzie softly said. "I'll bet that, once you move past the fact that he's a wolf that lives in the wild, he's really sweet."

"Sure," I grumbled while remembering how Snow had behaved like a domestic dog with both Oscar and Noah. Sinking against the back of the sofa, I asked, "Can he tell if a man is a werewolf or just a human?"

"Yes, he can," Noah said with confidence. "You couldn't have a better guardian. I guarantee it."

9

After raiding the outhouse that was in the opposite direction from the one I took when searching for it and placing the contents they'd removed from it in a hefty pile over the spot where I'd urinated, Oscar and Noah said their good-byes. Kenzie had been given last minute instructions and had audibly vowed to start out first thing with the intention of getting the job done in record time. Oscar vowed the same.

That night, I slept very little. Every sound in the night made me jump. With the moon on the verge of being full, it was bright enough for me to see the cabin's surroundings without the aid of a light. I periodically peered out of the window to search the tree line for a man who was really a werewolf come to steal me away.

I was still awake when I heard Kenzie clambering about the kitchen in an effort to get going for the day. It was obvious that she wasn't a morning person. I'd neglected to bring a robe. So, when I climbed out of bed,

I pulled on a cardigan to help ward off the early morning chill before joining my friend in the kitchen.

"I didn't mean to wake you," Kenzie apologized. "I'm not used to using a French press for my coffee. I dropped the kettle in the sink while filling it. My damned eyes always fight me when they first wake up."

"Your eyes or your hands?" I asked as I took the French press from her and measured the appropriate amount of coffee into it.

"I have poor depth perception when I first wake up. If that's not enough, my ever faithful arthritis likes to say good-morning," Kenzie lamented. "I slammed the kettle into the faucet and then my fingers gave out."

"I had no idea," I said with concern.

"I take meds to keep it under control," she explained. "By the time you see me, they've taken effect and I'm good to go."

"I don't usually see you until the afternoon," I said with concern. "It doesn't take that long, does it?"

She shook her head and murmured, "It takes about an hour," as she popped a few pills into her mouth and forced them down with a tall glass of water.

I watched her throat work at moving the pills and the water down into her esophagus until the glass was empty.

"Geez," I said in a voice just above a

whisper.

"Yep," she said as she caught her breath after holding it long enough to guzzle the water. "Every morning." Bending over the sink, she splashed water on her face several times before adding, "I don't need glasses. My vision is good. It's just that my eyes are lazy in the morning. Once I wake them up, I can see just fine."

"That's good," I said as I pulled the kettle off the stove and carefully poured the steaming liquid over the coffee grounds at the bottom of the French press. "This smells delicious."

"There's nothing better than a fresh cup of java in the morning," she said as she held her cup out for me to fill.

"We have to give it just a minute to brew," I explained. At the look of disappointment on her face, I said with assurance, "It will be well worth the wait. I promise."

"I want to get going within the next fifteen minutes," she nervously said. "I slept very little last night. I can't explain it, but my gut is telling me that we should get out of here before the full moon."

"You really believe what they said about the werewolves?" I asked.

She looked at me with concern as she said, "Normally, I'd say no, but I've never known Oscar to fabricate stories. Especially stories of such a nature. I was going to ask you what you think. I mean, what does your psychic think?"

"My psychic isn't alive to think," I said with irritation.

For some reason, it bothered me when people referred to my abilities as if they were independent entities. It happened more than I cared to admit, but it had never happened with Kenzie. I was a bit disappointed when it did.

"You know what I'm saying," she said with irritation. "It's morning and I'm waiting for coffee. Cut me some slack."

Feeling a bit better for that response, I smiled and said, "I don't really know. When the matter involves me, I have trouble deciphering. I will tell you that there is an energy coming from both brothers that is different and strong."

"Werewolf energy, maybe," she mused as she held her cup out for me to fill with the freshly brewed, aromatic liquid.

"Since I'm still debating about the existence of werewolves, I couldn't say," I replied. I could have told her that I'd also spent a night of hell worrying about werewolf men, but I didn't. Looking around the room I added, "Speaking of wolves, where's Snow?"

"He took off as soon as I went out to use the outhouse this morning," she replied as she lovingly cradled her coffee cup. "Damn, I love this stuff."

I poured coffee into a mug for myself and nodded. "I can't imagine starting the day without it." Feeling my bodily urges coming alive from the caffeine as I sipped my coffee, I added, "I need to use the outhouse. Seeing as Snow didn't feel the need to guard me, I'm assuming it's safe."

"It's beautiful out there already," Kenzie said with a nod. "You'll be shedding that sweater fast enough."

"Good," I said over my shoulder as I stepped out onto the porch. "I want to wash up in the lake. Warmth is good when you're using Mother Nature's supplies for cleaning up."

Her voice trickled out to me as I stepped off the porch as she chuckled and said, "So true. So true."

10

I relaxed on the porch and enjoyed the cabin's natural surroundings for an easy hour after watching Kenzie adjust her backpack as she hiked off into the woods to begin tagging duty. She was right about the weather. I'd shed my sweater almost immediately upon returning from using the outhouse. Sitting on the porch while reveling in the sensation of the faint warm breeze that caressed my flesh and feeling the heat of the morning sun on my face as it climbed higher over the treetops was so fantastic that I'd actually forgotten about Oscar and Noah's outrageous werewolf claims.

I'd also forgotten about Snow.

It wasn't until I was floating on my back in the clear lake water and spotted him sitting on shore near my clothes that I remembered the wolf. He looked so majestic as he sat watching my every move that it was almost breathtaking. Seeing how proud and tall he held himself also made me feel more at ease and protected enough to relax and enjoy my morning bath.

I reveled in my time in the water so much that I decided to hang out for as long as my body would allow. I'd been experiencing writer's block for some time, so I used the tranquility of floating aimlessly as a means to relax my mind enough to allow me to think on my story and possibly come up with the next writing installment.

With my eyes closed and the water lapping in and out of my ears, sounds from shore were faint and distant. Add to that the fact that my mind was working overtime going over the story that I was writing and it was easy to understand why I wouldn't have been aware of any warning from Snow that someone had arrived.

The feel of a strong, calloused hand on my bare shoulder brought me back to reality. Water rushed into my mouth as I gasped with surprise from the experience. Coughing to clear my air passages, I put my body upright as I whirled around to see who was in the lake with me.

With my arms working hard to keep me afloat, I first looked at the face that sneered at me from just a few feet away before I frantically searched for Snow. He was supposed to be my protector. Yet, here I was, naked in the lake, with an ugly and very creepy looking stranger a mere few feet away. So much for Noah's guarantee!

"Snow!" I choked out between coughs as I robotically moved my arms to keep my body upright and away from this frightening character.

"Is that his name?" the man asked with a deep, raspy voice that had a hint of growl in it. "He's fine. He's just been tranquilized."

"Tranquilized!" I exclaimed with dismay. I'd finally coughed away enough water to be able to breathe and talk. "Why?"

"So he wouldn't bite me, of course," the man said with humor.

Working my arms so that I was moving toward the shore while still looking at him, I asked, "Who are you?"

"I'm your future mate, little wolf," he replied.

My heart nearly stopped in my chest at his words before climbing into
my ears and beating against my eardrums. Not relying solely on my arms to get me to shore, I kicked my feet to aid in propelling me as far away from him as I could get as quickly as possible. I'd been on the swim team in high school. If ever there was a time to call upon that training, it was then. I was out of practice, but still good enough to get a bit of distance between him and me in a short period of time.

He called out, but I couldn't decipher

the words above the pounding in my ears combined with the gushing of the water as my body worked hard to get me as far from him as possible.

I climbed onto the shore just seconds before he did. Begging my legs to hold up under the unfamiliar stress that I'd put on them, I was almost to where Snow lay limp and peaceful when I felt his oversized, calloused hand grab my upper arm and yank me to a halt.

I was filled with so much fear and outrage that I actually forgot about the fact that I was completely naked.

"Let me go," I hissed as I tried to twist away.

Brown eyes that were set beneath thick, curly dark auburn eyebrows lit up with greed and lust as they studied every inch of my flesh.

"You look like you'll produce some mighty fine offspring," he said with satisfaction. "I was beginning to think I'd never find a mate. Times being like they are, and all. Sure, I could have gone with a human woman and produced a half-breed, but you're much better. You're sexy too."

It was at that moment that I realized that I wasn't the only one who was
naked. My captor also hadn't a stitch on. My eyes stared at his powerful looking upper arms before roaming over his barrel chest

that was covered with thick hair that matched his brows and then stopping at his sizable erection.

My gut told me that he intended on having his way with me whether he had my consent or not. My mind whirled over what to do. I was no virgin, but I also wasn't in the habit of having sex with perfect strangers, especially ugly ones. Not only was I repulsed by the thought, but it was clear that he intended to impregnate me.

I kicked at his shin so hard that my toes hurt and throbbed like I just might have broken them. It was enough of a surprise to get him to loosen his hold on my arm. Taking advantage of the moment, I twisted free and tried to scramble away. He simply threw his head back and emitted a deep graveling laugh as he lunged at me and forced me onto the ground with his own body weight. Searing pain shot through my chest as a loud crack assaulted my ears. I didn't need an x-ray to know that he'd cracked a rib when his bulk came crashing down on me.

The knowledge that I could puncture a lung if I moved in just the right way immediately subdued my efforts to be free. Lying only feet away from my unconscious protector, I allowed the tears to flow as my rapists hands roughly inspected my breast and then my womanhood.

"You're no virgin," he said in a low, rough tone as he slid his abrasive fingers deep into me. "That's fine. I wouldn't expect it. What matters is that you're still young enough to breed."

"Let me go," I frantically begged. "Let me go and I won't say a word about this."

"Go?" he said in a way that a predator might speak to its prey. "Go where, little wolf?"

"Don't call me that. I'm not a wolf," I hissed as he forced my legs open and settled himself between them.

"True. You ain't a wolf yet, but soon the moon will be full and I will turn you," he said as he rammed his manhood deep into me. "I'm just laying my claim onto you now before the others come looking for you."

Having his enormous erection shoved deep into my unprepared and unwanting womanhood was shockingly painful. I screamed loud and long as he pumped his manhood in and out of me; not just from the pain, but from the outrage of what was happening as well.

"You're hurting me!" I bellowed.

"Relax, little wolf," he urged with a deep throated voice as he continued to move in and out. "Relax and enjoy." Propping his torso onto his arms so that his weight wasn't on me, he said, "You're tight and dry. Here. Let me do this. It will help to loosen you up."

With that, his mouth attacked my breast. I squealed with disgust and pulled at his thick mass of unruly auburn hair in an effort to get him to stop suckling at my nipple. It was as if he was oblivious to the fact that he was only making matters worse. He moved his mouth from one breast to the other while never ceasing to assault me with his manhood.

When he finally gave my swollen, raw nipples a break, he held his torso off mine as he positioned himself to be able to drive his rod even deeper into me. It gave me a clear view of his ugly face. His skin was marked with the remnants of teenage acne and his nose was flat and crooked like he'd broken it one too many times. His hair was long, wild, and thick, giving it the appearance of a lion's mane around his broad face. His square jaw looked out of place beneath his thin lips. All in all, he had to be the ugliest man I'd ever laid eyes on.

And he was raping me.

I could feel his manhood growing. Since it looked overly engorged prior to him entering me, I was surprised by that fact. His breathing and grunting were indicating that he was just about to release his seed. The mere thought of this disgusting creature leaving a bit of himself in me made me shudder with revulsion and panic to the extent that I thought I'd go mad. Not knowing what else to do, I bit his wrist until I drew blood. He bellowed with anger and stopped pumping for a brief second, but quickly picked up where he left off.

I was at a loss over what to do. I'd managed to delay the inevitable by biting him, but not stop it. My mind had just begun running through the clinics that I could go to for the morning after pill when my assailant bellowed with despair as he was torn free of me.

My first thought was to see if he'd managed to release his seed. I didn't think he had, but I needed to be certain. I quickly felt between my legs for his semen. To my relief, there was none.

Feeling shaken but relieved that he hadn't had the chance to impregnate me, I focused on what was happening. Snow had awoken from his tranquilized state and come to my rescue. He'd torn into the man's shoulder when he pulled him off me and now had his fangs deep in my rapist's throat. As terrible as it was, I could feel no empathy for my assailant. As far as I was concerned, he deserved what the wolf was dishing out.

I sat in silent shock while I watched Snow hold tight to that ugly man's thick, muscled throat until he took his last breath. Instead of backing off, the beautiful beast continued to gnaw on my assailant's neck until he'd managed to sever his head from his body.

Still, I felt no emotion.

Nor did I budge. Not even an inch.

After picking up the man's head by his hair and tossing it a few feet from his body, Snow moved next to me and placed his bloody muzzle in my lap like a dog might a master. Half dazed and trembling from the adrenaline that was coursing through my veins and the trauma that I'd just endured, I robotically scratched his ears like I'd seen Noah and Oscar do while I remained ever silent.

I was still sitting on the ground with Snow's head in my lap when he perked up and gave a low growl. It quickly shifted to a growly bark as he stood up and took on a protective stance in front of me. With the wolf blocking my view, I wasn't able to see who or what was approaching. Terrified, I shrunk my body as small as I could get it behind my protector.

"Down boy," said a familiar male voice.

Snow immediately laid down on the ground in front of me as Noah steadily walked my way.

I stared at him with what I assume was a blank look as he assessed the situation. Seeing the naked, dead man with his head lying just feet away from him, he scowled.

"So, they've started to come," he grumbled. Reaching for my clothes, he picked them up and moved to hand them to me.

Panicked by his approach, I finally found my voice and shouted, "Keep away!"

He wore a shocked look as he stopped in his tracks. Then, taking a longer moment to study both my headless assailant and me, he closed his eyes and shook his head.

"I don't understand why Snow let him do that to you before taking him down," he said with an apologetic tone.

My voice trembled as I said, "He tranquilized Snow. I was swimming and he tranquilized Snow."

A gut wrenching groan came from his throat as he, once again, moved toward me.

"Stay away!" I screeched.

Tossing my clothes into my lap, he said, "Okay, but put these on."

It took longer than normal to dress as I struggled to stop the shaking. I hurt all over, especially in my chest. I could see visible bruises on my arms and legs as I carefully pulled on my top and shorts.

"I think he broke my rib," I said.

I wiped at blood from the corner of my mouth that I hadn't realized was there. With the adrenaline slowly leaving my system, I felt the full impact of the injuries I'd incurred during our struggle.

Getting onto my knees, I attempted to stand up. The searing pain in my chest brought tears to my eyes and my legs buckled beneath me. I cried out from the pain and frustration as I fell to the ground.

Ignoring my demands for him to stay away from me, he carefully cradled me in his arms and carried me back toward the cabin.

I felt a sudden sense of safety almost as soon as he pulled me close to him. So, rather than continuing to scream and rant for him to put me down, I wrapped my arms around his strong neck before burying my face into it and unabashedly crying my eyes out.

"I was raped by a man who said that he wanted to make me his mate," I finally choked into his flesh as my body shuddered. "He was big and ugly and Snow killed him."

"I'm so sorry," he said as he gently caressed my head and, then, lightly kissed it.

"If it wasn't for Snow...," I whimpered.

"He knew about Snow and was prepared for him," he grumbled with disappointment. "Damn."

"I need to be checked for diseases," I said with a touch of panic. "I need to be checked..."

"He wouldn't have a disease," he assured me. "Werewolves don't catch the STDs that humans pass around."

"He looked pretty human to me," I

murmured as my lips moved against the flesh of his strong neck that was wet and salty from my tears.

"He was, but he wasn't. It's that werewolf gene that makes the difference. We separate ourselves by referring to those who don't carry the gene as humans and us as werewolves," he explained. "Technically, I'm a human with a mutation. If you found my dead body and did an autopsy, you'd think I was simply human."

Finally lifting my face from his neck, I said, "It's scary, weird, and difficult to take in."

"Did he empty into you?" he asked with concern.

"I don't think so," I said. "I felt for something and it was dry. I'm so sore."

"Do you want to go back to the lake and soak?" he asked with concern.

I vigorously shook my head. I wasn't sure I'd ever be able to go back there.

"I think that a good soak would help you," he gently said. "Do you want to come to my home? I have a nice deep tub."

I thought for a moment before finally nodding. I didn't know how wise it was to go with him. He was someone else who I really didn't know. Yet, I felt safe at that moment. Whether a good soak would help me or not wasn't the reason I agreed to go. I wanted an opportunity to scrub that man away and I had no intention of going back to that lake.

Still in his strong arms with my slender ones wrapped around his neck in a vice-like grip, I said with a shaky voice, "I want to leave a note for Kenzie in case she comes back before we return."

Eileen Sheehan

11

With both of us lost in our own thoughts, the silence during Noah's and my trip off the mountain was acute. With my mind tortured by what had happened to me, I paid little attention to the drive or the time that it took.

When he pulled down a long, narrow drive that was lined by ancient and massive looking oak trees that mingled with balsom fir and white pine trees, I forced myself back to reality.

Positioned in the middle of a clearing that was circled by a thick mass of the same species of trees that lined the drive, his cedar sided house looked lonely, but majestic. The lawn was well manicured, but void of any shrubs or flowers. Since he was a busy man, it didn't surprise me that he'd kept the landscaping simple to care for.

Having met him at his rustic cabin and noticing the weathered cedar siding on the house, I was surprised to see how technically advanced his furnishings were. Being a fan of antiques and old homes, the décor wasn't for me, but it was impressive never-the-less.

He wasted no time in hustling me off to the ensuite bathroom attached to the guest room. It was an exact replica of his own private bath, complete with a deep jacuzzi tub. After making sure that I had all that I needed and would be okay on my own, he left to fetch me the morning after pill from a doctor friend of his. Even though I doubted I'd been impregnated, we both felt it better to be safe than sorry.

My huge sigh of relief was accompanied by a flooding of tears as I sank into the steaming water. Since I wasn't sure how badly broken my ribcage was, I decided to play it safe and not turn on the jets. Even without the massaging action that they would have provided, the water gave me a sense of solace and healing.

I spent the first part of my bath scrubbing at my flesh with a loofa and lavender scented soap until I could no longer feel the remnants of that evil man's assault on my body. After that, I simply sank as far down as I could and let the heat soak into my bones and calm my nerves. I wanted to wash away the visions I had of his ugly face hovering over mine while he drove himself deep into me without mercy every time I closed my eyes. To my dismay, as low into the depths of the water as I sank and as hard as I willed it, they just wouldn't go away.

The water was chilled and my flesh wrinkled like a one-hundred year old woman by the time Noah returned and called out for me to join him. It took me longer than I cared to admit to crawl out of the tub, but I eventually managed.

I'd just finished drying off when Kenzie bounded into the bathroom. It was then that I realized just how out of it I was that I wouldn't think to lock the door to a bathroom that belonged to a strange man while I took a bath.

"Dear god! Are you okay?" she bellowed as she rushed toward me with her arms opened wide.

I quickly backed away.

"My ribs hurt," I hurriedly explained. "I think one is broken."

"So Noah said," she muttered as she stood back and scowled. "We'll need to get an x-ray. The problem is that the guy's had his head torn off by a wolf. That's going to be tough to explain."

"Snow was protecting me," I protested.

She gave me a long serious look as she said in a soft voice, "If we tell the authorities what happened, they'll put Snow down."

I moaned with despair. The wolf had proven to be a loyal protector. Killing him for saving me was horrid to think about. It simply couldn't happen.

"Then, I'll say that I fell down the stairs or something," I grumbled.

"Except that I think it's best to have you examined for vaginal injuries," she explained. "I'm not pleased that Noah had you soak in a tub before you were examined, but it's done. You should still be checked out."

"Can't you do it?" I asked without thinking.

"I'm a vet, girlfriend," she said with a touch of humor. "Even if I was willing to look up in that thing, I'm not set up for it. We need a people doctor with the right equipment."

"What about the doctor friend that Noah went to for my morning after pill?" I hopefully asked.

"I thought of that," she said. "Then, I questioned if you'd be okay with it."

"Why not?" I asked with curious concern.

"He's a doctor, but he's also a member of Noah's pack," she replied.

"A werewolf?" I gasped.

Kenzie nodded.

I rested my backside against the edge of the tub and moaned. I'd allowed Noah to rescue me and had actually felt safe in his arms, but that didn't mean that I was ready to have another werewolf man touch my body. I especially wasn't sure I wanted him having access to my most intimate parts.

"I can take you to the hospital," Kenzie offered. "They'll have to be told about the rape and then there will have to be a police report filed..."

"No," I practically screeched out. "I won't have anyone killing Snow. He saved me. I owe him."

She heaved a sigh as she said, "It looks like it's Noah's doctor friend, then."

She needed to assist me in walking out to the main room of the house where Noah awaited. Now that I was clean and relaxed, my body wanted to simply rest. Asking it to move proved a daunting task.

Noah took one look at me struggling to make my way with Kenzie's help and snarled, "The bastard!"

"Is this the only incident we'll need to worry about?" Kenzie asked with concern. "I don't think she can survive another attack like this."

"The son-of-a-bitch was laying his claim on her. Had he lived, she'd have been deemed his and no other would bother her. Now that he's dead, she's fair game again," he said with regret.

"So, to lay a claim the werewolf man has to rape me?" I asked with dismay.

He shook his head as he said, "Not

rape you. He needs to have sex with you, though."

"Well, that can't happen," Kenzie said with conviction as she held me close. "It should have never happened to begin with. It most certainly won't happen again."

"They're crafty," Noah complained. "The guy tranquilized Snow to get to her. That wolf was my ace in the hand."

"How did he find out that you had Snow guarding her? I wonder," Kenzie mused.

Noah frowned as his eyes settled on me to the extent that I was uncomfortable and mused aloud, "That's a good question."

12

Dr. Mitchell Blake was a small, wiry man in his mid-fifties who looked like a perfectly normal man. Had I not known that he was one of Noah's pack, I'd never have guessed it. Then, I never would have thought Noah to be a werewolf either. The good doctor's appearance helped to lessen the trauma that I experienced at having to expose myself to a stranger for an intimate examination. His mild mannered politeness also didn't hurt.

"You're torn in two places," he informed me after completing my internal exam. "They aren't excessive, but I'm going to give you a cream to insert for the next few days. It will help to accelerate the healing process." As he turned his back to me and searched the cupboards for the medication that he wanted to supply me with, he added, "No sex until I've examined you again in two weeks."

"No worries there," I said with a trembling voice that refused to calm down no matter how hard I tried. "I'm not dating anyone."

He turned and looked at me with a serious, sad expression. After a short silence, he said, "I can't express my sorrow over what happened to you. We aren't all like that. I promise."

"People are people no matter who they belong to, I guess," I said in a voice that I barely recognized. "You find good and bad everywhere."

Heaving a small sigh, he pushed his thick rimmed glasses back up onto his nose before pulling out his script pad and scribbling something on it.

"You'll have to visit the pharmacy for this," he said as he ripped the sheet with the scribbling from the pad. "It's a mild sedative to help you relax. Your body is reacting to the trauma that it went through." Pulling out a syringe, he stuck the needle into a small vile while adding, "I'm going to give you a shot to get the process started, but I want you on that sedative for a few days at least."

Since my body refused to obey me and stop shaking, I didn't argue.

After giving me the shot and handing me a small bag with the cream I was to insert inside of me to help the healing process, he ordered me to get dressed in a gentle voice and then left the room.

Kenzie entered almost as soon as he'd

exited and assisted me with my clothes.

"If that son-of-a-bitch wasn't already dead, I'd kill him myself," she snarled as she slipped one pant leg and then the other onto me as if I was a child. I didn't resist her efforts as she pulled my jeans over my hips, zipped them up, and then fastened the waist. Hugging me as tightly as she dared, she asked with a gentle, caring tone, "Did he say you broke a rib?"

"A slight fracture," I said with a nod. "It should be okay in a few weeks."

"Damn!" she snarled with frustration.

"He was big and heavy," I explained. "When he pounced on me to hold me down, he used all of his body weight."

"I'll bet you were a wildcat," she said with pride.

"Not after I heard the crack and felt the pain," I admitted. "I was too concerned about a rib puncturing my lung or something equally as bad
happening."

"Smart thinking," Kenzie said. "It's damned lucky that the fool miscalculated Snow's body weight and the sedative wore off sooner than he expected."

"Lucky for me," I wistfully said, "but not for him."

"He deserved what he got," she grumbled as she moved toward the door. "Are you ready?"

I nodded and followed her out of the examination room and into the waiting room where Noah and Dr. Blake were waiting.

Noah's face was white with rage as he listened to the whispers of his doctor friend. He looked directly at me with his eyes, but I could tell that he wasn't seeing me. He was seeing something in his mind that angered him.

Holding out the script that the doctor had given me, I said, "I need to go to the pharmacy and get this filled."

"You need to go to bed," Noah said with firm authority. "I will go to the pharmacy."

"I can do it," Kenzie said as she snatched the script from my hand. "I want her to be watched by someone who is capable of protecting her at all times."

With a long look and nod between Kenzie and Noah, she thanked the doctor for helping and headed out the front door. With the sedative taking effect, I had no desire to stop her. In fact, I didn't want to do much of anything except close my eyes and sleep.

I was only vaguely aware of Noah carefully cradling me in his arms and carrying me toward the back part of his house. I couldn't help comparing it with the rough and ready way in which he'd carried me from the forest while arguing with his brother about my peeing in the woods. The difference was night and day.

"You'll be safe back here," he said as he gently laid me onto a king sized bed.

I let out a soft moan at how good the mattress felt beneath me. Thinking that he hurt me as he'd set me down, he hurriedly apologized.

"No. No," I protested with a weak, but steadier voice than I'd had since the attack. "I moaned because it feels so good, not because it hurt. This mattress feels like heaven."

He gave a small chuckle, but said nothing more.

I watched through half-closed eyelids as he sauntered toward the bedroom door. Even after all I'd been through and being sedated, I couldn't help responding to the virile image he displayed. His perfect lean and muscled body moved with a rugged confidence that shouted super stud. I wondered if he realized just how sexy he was.

"Probably," I said aloud without realizing it.

He stopped and turned to look at me. With a raised brow, he repeated the word. "Probably?"

I sucked in air as I chastised myself for not being in control of my mouth. It had to be the shot that I'd been given. Not knowing what to say or do, I rolled onto my side and muttered, "I'm probably safe."

"You're definitely safe, sleeping beauty," he said in a low tone. "I intend to watch over you myself until I can no longer do it."

I turned and looked at him with wavering eyesight.

"When is that?" I heard myself ask in a faraway voice.

"The full moon," he replied.

No longer able to resist the sedative, I closed my eyes and let my woes float into nothingness.

13

It was dark when I felt someone's weight lowering onto the mattress beside me. Still groggy, I was only vaguely aware of the fact that Noah was now sharing the king sized bed with me.

"You're in my bed," I drowsily slurred.

"Actually," he said with a low, soft tone, "you're in mine."

Forced into a slightly more coherent state from the surprise of discovering that I'd been sleeping in his bed for the better part of the day, I said with dismay, "This is your bed? I'm in your bed?"

"There's no need to panic," he assured me. "I want to keep you close. It makes sense to put you next to me during the night. This is the most vulnerable time."

Hearing his words, I moved a little closer to him. My body was still trembling. I wasn't sure if it was still the remnants from the attack or from the reality of the situation that he'd just pointed out.

"You are safe," he said with assurance.

"Go back to sleep."

"I'm frightened," I confessed in a low whisper.

Pulling me close to him, he wrapped me in his arms and said, "Don't be. I've got you."

"What about Snow?" I timidly asked. "Where's Snow?"

The bed was positioned in the room in such a way that the light of the moon fell onto his face. My heart skipped a beat as I admired his handsome
features while he emitted a faint chuckle.

"So, he's you're buddy now?" he asked with a touch of humor in his voice.

"I'd just feel better if he was near," I admitted.

"He's right outside the door," he said. "Now, go to sleep."

"Can he come in the room with us?" I persisted.

"Damn, woman," he grumbled as he sat up and swung his legs over the edge of the bed.

With the approaching full moon lighting up the night through the large picture window in his bedroom, it was easy to see his strong back and arms as he moved toward the door to summon Snow into the room. With my vision still under the influence of the sedative, the world felt surreal. Even so, my eyes couldn't resist tracing the silhouette of the muscles that rippled down his back until they rested on a well-formed buttocks that wore only a pair of terry jockey shorts. I sucked in air at the sight of his tight, muscular thighs working to bring him back to the bed.

As he slid back under the covers, I couldn't help comparing him with the ugly beast who'd raped me. I found myself wondering if I'd have resisted the man if he'd looked like Noah.

Shocked at my own thoughts, I chastised myself before pardoning my shameful thinking as a side effect of the medication I'd been given.

After checking to make sure of Snow's exact location in the room, I settled back down. He'd positioned himself on the floor on my side of the bed. It was enough to remove the tremors that had overtaken my body and replace them with a calm, confidence.

Without asking permission, or saying anything at all, Noah reached for me once more. Wrapping me in his arms again, he pulled me close as he settled in for the night.

I gave him no argument as I rested my head on his chest and let the rhythm of his beating heart lull me back to sleep.

When I awoke again, the sun was shining bright through the window to the extent that it hurt my eyes. Keeping them only half opened to prevent the pain from returning, I searched the bed for Noah with both my eyes and my hands.

He was gone.

"Noah?" I hesitantly called out in a soft tone. "Noah, are you here?"

"I'm here," he informed me as he entered the room with a bed tray containing a French press with freshly brewed coffee and a toasted bagel. "I didn't know what you ate in the morning," he said with a grin. "Then, it wouldn't really matter because all I have is coffee and bagels."

Wincing as I sat up, I did my best to position myself in the bed so that he could set the bed tray over my legs. I was both surprised and disappointed to discover that I was in even more discomfort than I'd been the day before.

"It's normal to feel everything the following day," he explained. "The adrenaline is leaving your body. That's what kept the pain at bay."

"I'd rather it stayed," I grumbled.

"It was also what made you tremble like you were," he continued. "I can see from here that you're hands are much steadier."

He was right, of course. I was feeling more pain, but less tremors.

"The pain will subside in a few days," he offered. "It will lessen after you've taken your meds too."

"I don't want more of that sedative," I

complained as I remembered my lusty thoughts of him the night before.

"Normally, I'd say that you don't have to, but, in this case, I think it's best that we follow the doctor's orders," he replied.

"They make my mind muddled," I whined.

"They're supposed to," he said with a grin as he held out two pills and a small glass of water to wash them down with.

I frowned with disappointment at the idea of being forced to take a medication that I didn't want to take. Seeing my expression, he sat on the edge of the bed and lowered his hands to his lap.

"Listen," he said with a serious tone. "I don't want to force you to take these pills and I won't. It's just that both the doc and I think it's best if you were kept in a relaxed and sedated state for the next few days. You have a cracked rib that needs you to stay still so that it can heal correctly and you've been traumatized. I imagine that if you don't take the meds, you'll only fret and worry over when the next attack will occur. That won't help you heal and it won't help me keep you safe."

"How would my worrying prevent you from keeping me safe?" I asked with genuine curiosity.

"I'd be preoccupied with your fears instead of with your safety," he explained.

It suddenly dawned on me just how much of a burden I was placing on a man I barely knew. Rather than fight him, I should have been thanking him and cooperating. Feeling ashamed, I held out my hand to accept the medication and the water.

"I don't mean to be such trouble," I said. "I can go somewhere else. This is a lot to ask of you when you don't even know me."

He vigorously shook his head.

"You will stay right here," he firmly commanded. "If you hadn't gone to my cabin, you'd have probably gone through life never knowing of the existence of werewolves or that you carry the gene and they'd never know about you. It's Oscar's and my fault that you're in this mess and we'll see that you get out of it."

"Is Oscar here?" I asked as I looked toward the door.

What I interpreted as a look of jealous disappointment swept over his face before he was able to regain control of his expression.

"You like Oscar, eh?" he asked with a controlled voice.

I shrugged as I said, "He seems nice enough. Kenzie trusts him and that's good enough for me."

"I see," he said as he watched me swallow my medications and then positioned the tray over my legs.

Having caught his brief look of jealousy, my heart skipped a beat. Could it be that this sex god was actually insecure? Better yet. Could it be that he liked me enough to be jealous and insecure?

Not able to resist the temptation to press the issue, I asked, "Why else would I ask for him?"

To my disappointment, his face remained stoic as he replied, "Since you don't know him any better than you do me, I was just surprised to hear you ask for him. That's all."

"If you want to get technical, I didn't ask for him," I said with a touch of irritation. "I asked if he was here. There's a difference."

He gave me a heart melting smile as he said, "Yes, there is."

I snarled inwardly at his back as he left the room. I was certain that he'd displayed jealousy over my asking if Oscar was around. Could my mind be playing tricks on me again? I cursed myself for taking more of that medication as I resigned myself to the fact that I was stuck in that bed until my ribs would allow me out of it.

14

Inserting the cream that the doctor sent home with me proved to be more difficult than I'd expected. The pain in my ribs and my fear of making matters worse prohibited me from being as flexible as I needed to be in order to do it properly. I was still struggling with maneuvering my body to better accept the applicator when Kenzie knocked on the bathroom door.

"Are you okay in there?" she asked with a concerned tone. "Noah tells me that you've been in here for some time."

"He noticed I went to the bathroom?" I cried with disbelief. "Is there no privacy in this house?"

"Not if you want to stay safe, there isn't," she replied. "What's going on. Do you need help?"

I hesitated for a moment before giving in and telling her that I did indeed need help. When she entered the room and I explained why her assistance was required, I regretted not having a camera. The look on her face when I told her that she would have to insert the cream into my vagina was absolutely priceless.

"I didn't think you'd be squeamish about something like this. You are a doctor, after all," I teased.

"As I've already pointed out, I'm an animal doctor, not a people doctor," she replied. Then, after an enormous sigh of resignation, she snatched the applicator from my hand. "Give me that and spread your legs," she ordered. After inserting the cream, she looked me in the eye and said with a firm tone, "Never speak of this. Understand?"

I giggled and nodded. It was unusual to see my self-confident, save all the animals on the planet friend so thrown off kilter by something that I'd expected her to do without a hitch.

"You seem okay with having me touch you," she observed as she tossed the disposable applicator into the garbage can.

"Shouldn't I be?" I asked with confusion as I carefully adjusted my clothes in preparation for leaving the bathroom.

"It's just that a good many rape victims are left scarred and resistant to being touched afterwards," she explained.

"I'm scarred in some ways, but I'm also tough," I said with assurance. "Besides, you aren't a man or a werewolf and you'd never hurt me."

"No, I would not," she said with resignation as she went to the sink to wash and dry her hands. "This medication will have to be applied for some time. A few days, at least. I'll have to do it for you until your ribs let you do it yourself."

"Maybe tomorrow will be better," I hopefully said.

"That would be nice, but I'll come around just in case," she said as she opened the door and motioned for me to go through it with a sweep of her arm.

I kept walking until I reached the kitchen where I found Noah sitting at his kitchen table with a steaming cup of coffee in front of him.

Seeing me enter, he jumped to his feet.

"I have fresh coffee in the pot," he said with what I perceived might be a nervous voice, but, since I didn't know him I couldn't be sure. "Kenzie brought some danish."

I was filled with mixed emotions as I sat down at the table and joined my host and my friend for a fresh cup of coffee and an absolutely delicious cheese danish.

Kenzie wasn't totally off the mark when she spoke of rape victims being damaged from the attack. The mere thought of having a man touch me in an intimate way made me shudder with dread. Yet, I experienced emotions that I hadn't felt about the opposite sex... ever... whenever I looked at Noah. These contradicting feelings were made even more taxing for me to deal with by the sedative that I foolishly took another dose of and that was starting to hit me full force.

Noah looked at me with an expression that I simply couldn't decipher no matter how hard I tried before turning to Kenzie and saying, "Your friend is starting to feel the sedative that Mitch prescribed. I can see it in her eyes. She resisted taking it. I didn't force her, but I was glad when she finally decided to take it."

My good friend smiled as she said, "That doesn't surprise me. Lisa's not big on drugs. She's basically a naturalist."

"She's also in a lot of pain," he offered. "The sedative works on both nerves and pain. I think it's best she takes it as prescribed until she's better."

Kenzie nodded.

"You're probably right," she agreed. "My girl is a tough one, but what she endured goes beyond what should happen to anyone. I'm thinking that the aftershock of what happened hasn't hit her yet."

"I'm right here, you know," I said with groggy annoyance.

"Yes, you are when you should be in bed," Noah said with an authoritative tone.

"If that's true, why did you have me sit

down for coffee and a danish?" I asked with a touch of contempt.

He shrugged as he said, "I'm not sure except that it seemed the thing to do at the time. Now, thinking better of it, I should have turned you around right away."

I indignantly pushed my chair back from the table and stood up.

"Don't worry, I'm going," I snipped.

I took a step and my legs buckled. My eyes went wide with surprise as I fell to my knees.

"Damn!" Noah bellowed as he rushed to my side.

"Lisa!" Kenzie exclaimed as she hurried to support me by my shoulders until Noah was able to pick me up and cradle me in his arms.

"I should have known better than to bring her out here. It's my fault," Kenzie moaned as she followed Noah into the bedroom.

Although I was annoyed with my body for failing me, I was also a little worried. I'd always considered myself strong and healthy. Yet, I was having an extremely difficult time functioning. Was it simply the side effect of the medication? Or, was there more damage to my body than any of us realized?

I wanted to express my fears to Kenzie, but she hovered beside Noah while they settled me back into bed and left with him. I'm not sure why I didn't want him to hear my concerns, but I didn't.

Closing my eyes, I told myself that I could discuss things with my friend later and gave way to sleep.

I awoke several times during the day to find Noah by my side with food and medication for me to force down. I wasn't allowed enough coherency to find it in me to resist, so I simply swallowed whatever he happened to put into my mouth.

I remember wondering who the cook was. He'd only had bagels to offer me for breakfast, yet he was carefully spooning a delicious soup into my mouth that I just couldn't get enough of. I thought to ask him on several occasions if it was he who'd managed to put such a tasty dish together or if he'd gotten carry out, but I never did get around to it before my satisfied stomach lulled me back to sleep like a baby.

When he climbed into bed next to me that night, I felt safe and secure. I willingly let him pull me close like he'd done the night before. Whether Snow was in the room or not, I couldn't tell. Since I was at a point of not caring, I didn't ask. Instead, I inhaled the musky, manly scent of my protector while I, once again, allowed the steady beat of his heart to lull me back to slumber land.

15

When I awoke the following morning, there was no sign of Noah. Since he'd risen before me the day before, I didn't think much of it. Instead, I settled back into the pillows while I waited for him to arrive with coffee and a bagel, as he'd done the morning before. To my surprise, he didn't come.

I waited for half an hour before I climbed out of bed and went to the bathroom to relieve myself. I was surprised at how comfortable I was wandering about in the bra and panties that I'd slept in. I couldn't explain it even to myself, but Noah's house felt like home to me.

After taking the time to brush my teeth, wash the sleep from my face, and eliminate my bedhead hairdo, I pulled on my shorts and a tee shirt and headed out of the bedroom in search of him.

Although I felt more alert from the hours of sleep that I'd had, I was still feeling the effects of the sedative. The world had a touch of surrealism to it and my legs were unstable. I held the wall and various pieces of furniture to help me stay both grounded and upright as I slowly made my way out of the bedroom.

"She's up," I heard a familiar male voice say when I entered the living room. It wasn't Noah's voice, but my muddled mind knew that I'd heard it before.

Kenzie rushed to my side and aided me into the nearest easy chair.

"I was just going in to check on you," she said as she examined my eyes with her own. "I'm not sure you should be taking any more of that sedative. You have the eyes of a druggie."

"I wanted to stop yesterday," I complained. "It's too strong for me."

"I think I might have to agree with you there," she said with a nod. "Other than drugged out, how are you feeling? How are your ribs?"

"They feel better, but I should probably play it safe for one more day and get help with," I began as I looked around the room to see who else was with us. Seeing both Noah and Oscar, I whispered the rest of my sentence, "you know."

"Let's get you fed first and then we can take care of that," she said with a motherly tone.

"I'm not really hungry," I said, "but it's good to be out of bed."

"You slept a long time," Oscar said from across the room. "Almost a full twenty-four hours."

"It's the drugs your brother and his doctor friend insisted I take," I complained.

"You needed to sleep to heal," Noah protested. "I'm not going to apologize."

"No," Kenzie quickly interjected. "Nor should you. I agree that our girl needed to sleep, but I think we can ease up on the sedative now."

"What about tonight? Is she up to the trip?" Oscar asked as he moved across the room and stood next to Kenzie.

"What?" I asked with confusion.

Kenzie scowled at Oscar as if she disapproved of his bringing it up at that time before looking at me and saying, "We need to move you to somewhere safe for tonight and tomorrow night. That's why we're hoping your ribs are a little better."

"Why do I need to move?" I asked with a hint of panic.

The aftershock of the rape was finally settling in. I felt safe and secure in Noah's home. The thought of leaving my sanctuary was almost terrifying.

"I was afraid this might happen," Kenzie warily said. "I was actually waiting for it."

"Waiting for what?" Oscar asked.

"Aftershock," Kenzie said with a firmness. "Posttraumatic stress. She's been traumatized, remember? We don't just have to worry about her physical body if we want to move her. We have to think about her emotions as well."

"It's the full moon tonight and tomorrow night," Noah explained in a gentle voice. "Remember? I told you that I couldn't be with you during the full moon. I turn. So does Oscar. We need to put you somewhere safe."

"Would you hurt me if you turned?" I asked with both curiosity and concern.

His shocked look was mirrored by both Oscar and Kenzie.

"You can't possibly want to stay with him while he's a werewolf," Kenzie said in a low voice that was meant for my ears, but I guessed that they heard as well.

Looking directly at Noah, I asked, "Where do you plan on taking me?"

"We're still deciding," he said with a scowl.

"My brother manages to find fault with every place we suggest," Oscar pointed out.

With my eyes locked on Noah, I asked again, "Would you hurt me when you turned?"

He looked away and slowly shook his head.

"Then, I'll stay right here if you're good

102

with that," I said with conviction.

"You don't know what you're saying," Kenzie gasped. "He turns into a werewolf, Lisa. Have you ever seen a werewolf?"

"Have you?" I challenged. "A real one, that is. Not something from the movies."

"No, I haven't," she replied. Then, giving Oscar an apologetic look, she added, "I'm not sure I'd want to."

I turned to Oscar and asked, "What about you? Would you hurt me?"

He shook his head and said, "I wouldn't touch you, but you'd probably be scared to death from the look of us. We aren't pretty."

"She can't stay here if you don't stay too," Noah said with a gentle firmness to Kenzie. "When Oscar and I turn, we'll want to run off the excess energy. During that time, she'd be vulnerable. She'd need an extra pair of eyes to help keep an eye out for intruders."

"I'm no bodyguard," Kenzie complained.

"No, but Snow is," Noah continued. "We'd just need you to be his backup."

"We turn into a werewolf, but we're still coherent and function as a human with speech and actions. They're just more aggressive. It's not like in the movies where they wake up not knowing what they've done. We know exactly what we've done,"

Oscar said. Handing Kenzie a small beeper, he added, "Both Noah and I will keep one on us. If you suspect trouble, just push the button and we'll come back."

"Do you have to go out for a run after you turn?" I asked with the hope that they'd say "no".

Unfortunately, they didn't.

"Running burns off the animal energy. If we don't run for the first hour or so, we find it difficult to control the animal urges in us," Noah explained. "It's a trick that our ancestors discovered to help them coexist with humans. We run and then lock ourselves behind closed doors until the sun comes up."

"Not all werewolves do that," Oscar added. "In fact, most don't. They think that it's necessary to remain in the wild and connect with their beastly side until they turn back. That's when they get into trouble. The longer they stay out in nature while in that state, the greater the chances their animal urges have of overriding their humanity. It can get pretty messy."

I looked at my friend with seriousness and asked, "I don't expect you to stick around and share a house with two werewolves, but can you handle a few hours alone with me and Snow?"

16

We sat on the front porch of Noah's cedar sided house and watched as the sun slowly slid behind the treetops that bordered his property.

"How much longer before you turn?" I asked as I looked directly at Oscar.

I couldn't explain why, but I was avoiding looking at Noah. I inwardly thought that it was because I didn't want to witness his handsome face turning beastly. Since I had no feelings for Oscar, other than the fact that he seemed like a nice person, I assumed that it wouldn't affect me as much.

"It won't be long now," Oscar replied as he moved next to Kenzie and asked, "Do you want to go inside before it happens?"

She looked from Oscar, to Noah, and then to me before saying, "I believe I would."

"Kenzie?" I said with surprise.

Oscar raised his hand and shook his head.

"It's okay," he said with a soft voice. "I'm not offended. I completely understand."

"Well, I don't," I barked as I glowered at my friend. "Whether you have the face of a wolf or of a man, you're still who you are. I think you should be supported, not shunned."

Oscar gave a warm smile as he said, "That's nice."

"Okay," Kenzie reluctantly said as she plopped into the chair next to mine.

"Seriously, Kenz," Oscar said with a scowl. "You don't need to stay and watch. It won't hurt my feelings."

"Apparently it will hurt Lisa's," she grumbled.

"You're the vet, yet I'm the one who's willing to stay and watch," I said with surprise.

"What does being a vet have to do with any of this?" she almost screeched.

"Go inside, Kenzie," Noah said with a firm voice that sounded much deeper than normal. "Go now."

"It's happening, isn't it?" she nervously asked.

"It is," Oscar said in an equally altered voice.

"Both of you, go inside," Noah aggressively barked.

"But...," I began.

"Now!" he bellowed.

We didn't waste a moment before our

feet carried us into the house. Slamming the door shut behind us, Kenzie leaned against it. She was breathing heavy and her eyes were closed. I could see a vein in her neck throbbing as her racing heart pumped blood through it.

"Kenzie?" I softly said as I rested my hand on her arm.

She vigorously shook her head as a lone tear slid down her cheek.

"You can't possibly understand," she muttered. "I have known Oscar for years. He's very dear to me. More than I realized, in fact. I don't want that to change."

"And you think that by seeing him shift it would?" I asked.

She quietly nodded.

I thought for a moment before saying, "If you really care for him, it shouldn't matter. What if he was caught in a fire and his face was disfigured? Would you stop caring for him?"

"Of course not," she snapped.

"Well, then?" I said.

She opened her eyes and looked at me.

"But, a werewolf?" she protested.

"It could be worse," I replied.

"How?" she asked.

I shrugged as I flippantly said, "He could be a vampire. Those fangs would make kissing quite awkward."

After staring at me with disbelief for a moment, she burst into laughter.

"I needed that," she said as she left the door and walked to the window.

"What are you doing?" I asked as I followed her.

"Seeing if I can catch a glimpse of them before they head off to the woods," she replied.

"I like that idea," I said as I peered out the window. "After all, we want to make sure we recognize them when they come back."

"If we didn't, Snow would," she said.

"True," I said, "but I'd just feel better if I did too."

We managed to catch them in their final stage of transformation. I found it fascinating.

"This isn't scary at all," I said.

"No," she said with breathy awe. "It's actually quite beautiful."

I watched with wonder as the handsome human faces of the two brothers transformed into equally handsome wolf faces. Their bodies morphed into large, bulky, hairy versions of themselves. Had it been Halloween, they could have easily passed for men in costumes.

"I didn't think that Oscar could be more good looking, but, by golly, I think he is," she gasped.

"Spoken like a true animal lover," I

giggled.

She smiled.

"Come on," she said. "Are you going to tell me that you don't find Noah to be easy on the eyes?"

"In which form?" I asked with a teasing voice.

She studied me before excitedly saying, "You like him."

I could feel my face turning color as I looked away.

"There's no shame in that," she assured me. "I think it's wonderful. I was beginning to worry about you. Celibacy is unhealthy. To have what happened to you after years of it... well, let's just say that I was worried that you'd never give a man a chance again."

"We haven't done anything," I quickly said.

"I should hope not," she replied. "If Noah is anything like Oscar, he'd respect the fact that you're in recovery."

I nodded.

"He's held me close while I sleep," I offered. "That's all."

"That's enough to create a bond," she said with satisfaction. "The rest will come in time. You take as long as you want."

"You act as if you know that he wants me," I said with a touch of hopefulness.

"He'd be crazy not to," she said.

"Besides, I'm not blind. I see the way his eyes follow your every move."

"He feels guilty about having me go to their cabin," I said. "He said that, if he and his brother hadn't let me go there, I'd have gone through life not ever knowing about werewolves or them knowing about me."

"You don't know that," she snipped. "You can't tell the future like that." Then, remembering that I was psychic, she added, "Or, maybe you could."

"Not really," I said. "I have to be in danger or something and, then, I have to have some bit of information about the situation so that I can decipher what I'm feeling. I felt apprehension when I met both Oscar and Noah, but I would have never guessed it was because they were werewolves."

"Why did you think that you felt it?" she asked with earnest.

I looked down and grinned.

"I didn't know with Oscar, but when I met Noah, I thought it was because I found him sexy and that hasn't happened in a very long time," I said.

"You didn't find Oscar sexy?" she said with surprise.

"I did, but I also knew that he was off limits," I replied.

"He's my friend, Lisa," she insisted. "He's not off limits."

"Tell him that," I said with a chuckle.

17

We spent the next few hours drinking wine and playing cards. I'd never played rummy, but I found myself to be quite good at it. I enjoyed Kenzie's frustration over what she called 'beginner's luck' so much that I actually forgot where I was or that the moon was full and I was technically in danger. It wasn't until Snow stood at attention and snarled that it all came rushing back to me.

I froze in dumb terror as I watched Kenzie slam her cards on the kitchen table where we'd been playing and push herself off of the chair. Moving with rapid stealth, she went to the window and peered out from behind the closed curtains.

"I don't see anyone," she said in a hushed tone.

Finally regaining my wits, I raced to Noah's bedroom to get a view of the back part of the house. The bright moonlight made visibility easy as I scoped the landscape through the bedroom window. I was about to give up searching with my eyes when I spotted movement off in the tree-line.

"Kenzie," I said with a projected hushed voice. "There's someone in the trees!"

My heart passed through my throat until it settled in my head and beat against my brain. I had so much adrenaline coursing through my veins that it was difficult to think, let alone keep my body from shaking.

Kenzie came up behind me and placed a firm hand on my shoulder. It was enough reassurance to make the pounding in my head settle down so that I could hear her words and my body relax enough to prevent the heart attack that I was certain was about to happen.

"Show me," she softly said in my ear as she rested her chin on my shoulder.

I pointed in the direction of the trees where I'd seen movement with a trembling finger.

Rushing to the closet, she pulled out a long red cape. Tossing it over my shoulders, she adjusted the hood over my head.

"Noah told me about this," she quickly explained. "Apparently, werewolves can't see red. It's the same with some animals, so I believe him. He told me to cover you with this if we saw someone other than them around the house."

"Will this keep them away?" I nervously

asked as I pulled the sides of the cape closed in my front.

She shook her head.

"They'll be able to see your form. It's got Noah's scent on it, but I imagine they might still smell a hint of you. It will at least help to keep your identity somewhat hidden until Oscar and Noah return," she said. "I hit the beeper. Since they've been gone almost two hours, I suspect they're close."

"I sure hope so," I said as I rushed to Snow's side and sat on the floor next to him. "Maybe, if I stay close to Snow, his scent will help cover mine."

"That's good thinking. Even so, I think that you and Snow should go into the basement," she said. "There are too many windows in this house for my liking."

"I'm claustrophobic," I abashedly admitted. "Is there an exit from the basement? I'll be okay if there is an exit."

"I'm not sure," she admitted. "Even if there isn't, I think you're better off down there."

I reluctantly followed her advice.

Since it wasn't apparent from the front of the house that there even was a basement, I was surprised to discover that it was a finished one. Not only was there an exit, but it was a sliding glass door leading out to the back lawn that sloped into a mini valley behind the house.

"This won't be much help in protecting us if they decide to come in," I said to my guardian wolf as I made certain that the door was locked and the blinds were closed.

Sitting on the sofa, I motioned for Snow to position himself close to me while I listened to Kenzie rushing about overhead as she checked the locks on the doors and windows. He placed his muzzle in my lap like he'd done near the lake after beheading my attacker. It gave me enough of a sense of security to keep my mind thinking rationally and my ears hearing clearly.

While I affectionately caressed the wolf's head, I studied the basement for places that would be good to hide in, should the need arise. There was a wet bar with a closet behind it, but that seemed too obvious. There was also a closet near the exit. Again... too obvious. I was just beginning to feel the frustration of defeat when I spotted a barely visible knob in the paneling near the floor. Not only did its color blend with the wall, but it was small; the type of pull knob that you'd expect to see on a dresser drawer or a cabinet.

When I moved to the wall and carefully pulled at it a narrow panel glided open, exposing a small cubby. Just big enough for one, possibly two people, it was a good hiding place for sure. Knowing that I'd risk hyperventilating if I had to seek refuge in it, I kept it as a last resort.

Huddling back on the sofa with my arms around Snow's neck, I closed my eyes and listened to the silence of the house. Kenzie had stopped walking around. I shuddered from the creepiness I felt in a dwelling that only minutes before seemed like home.

My entire body jolted to attention when I heard Kenzie bellow the words, "Get out!"

They were quickly followed by thuds, thumps, crashes, and howls.

I wasn't able to make out how many werewolves were fighting upstairs, but I knew that there was more than one.

Snow growled and I worriedly did my best to hush him. As it was, I feared for Kenzie's wellbeing. I didn't need my wolf protector to bring attention to our whereabouts on top of it.

When Kenzie shouted, "Oscar, look out!", a wave of relief swept over me. She was right about them being nearby. The two brothers had responded to her summons in record time and were now tending to the intruder or intruders.

When silence returned to the house, I waited for a few minutes before creeping my way up the stairs. I'd just pushed the basement door open enough to peer out when I heard Noah's deepened voice tell Kenzie to keep me downstairs.

My friend readily responded and ushered me back into the basement.

"It's a bloody mess up there," she explained. "Apparently, the only way to kill a werewolf is to behead it. I guess Noah wants to keep you from seeing that."

"Too late," I muttered as I followed her back down the stairwell. "Snow took the head off my attacker. Remember?"

"I do," she replied. "Even so, I can understand him wanting to spare you from seeing any more. I deal with blood every day and it still grossed me out. The fact that it was done by the two brothers made it especially potent."

Once into the basement, she gave a look of approval.

"Not what I expected," she said with a smile. "I was thinking more creepy root cellar. This is more of a gaming room."

"Yes, it's nice, but also not super safe," I said as I pointed to the sliding glass door.

"I see," she murmured. "I imagine when he built this it wasn't with protecting damsels from werewolves in mind."

"Maybe," I said as I moved to the hidden cubby and opened it. "Although, there's this."

Kenzie chuckled, "Your man is clever."

"My man?" I said with surprise. "We barely know each other."

"Tell that to him," she giggled.

18

We remained in the basement while the men cleaned up and made sense of the main house after the battle. It turned out that there were three werewolves come to fetch me back to their pack. I could only imagine the mess the fighting created.

"How badly did they destroy his house?" I asked.

Even though the décor wasn't my taste, it was a beautiful home. I felt horrible that I was the reason for any destruction that occurred while protecting me.

"They broke a few things, but it's mostly the bodies and blood that need to be cleaned up," she replied. "I'm going to go up and see if they want our help."

I nodded as I watched her climb up the stairwell. Within seconds, she was back down relaying the fact that they would appreciate it if we just stayed in the basement until morning.

Since there was a futon sofa, a recliner, and a television, we made ourselves comfortable. Admittedly, I felt a bit guilty watching sitcoms while they were cleaning up dead bodies, but I also knew that neither Noah or Oscar would have been happy with us sitting downstairs fretting over the situation. Concentrating on the television shows aided in relaxing us enough so that we finally passed the remainder of the night in slumber.

Noah's hand gently shaking me awake was actually comforting. Wiping the sleep from my eyes, I adjusted the recliner that I'd opted to spend the night in into the upright position and accepted the steaming mug of fresh coffee that he was offering.

"How are you doing?" he asked as he gently brushed stray hairs from my face and secured them behind my ear.

The act was so loving and intimate that I forgot that we'd really only met a few days earlier. Taking his hand in mine, I held it to my cheek.

"Last night was just the beginning," he said with a tone of dismay as he gently retrieved his hand. "They'll be even more aggressive tonight. We'll have to think of a better way to protect you."

With sleep finally leaving my eyes enough for me to focus, I gasped at the sight of a large gash on his neck. It looked like someone had taken a set of claws and drawn them across his flesh from his ear to his collar bone.

"You're hurt," I said as I set my coffee mug onto the side table next to my chair and stood up to get a better look. "Let me see."

He stepped back a few feet.

"I'm good," he said. "It's just a scratch."

"The hell it is," I grumbled as I pushed forward until I was standing only inches from him.

My body fluttered inside from the nearness. All thoughts of the tragic attack on my person that occurred only days earlier flew out of my mind. They were replaced by brief images of making love with him.

I hoped that the chills of desire that roamed my physique weren't visible. Never had a man had such an effect on me. It was both exciting and disturbing.

His smell had changed. I still recognized his manly musk, but it was mixed with another familiar scent. It took a minute, but I finally realized that it was the same scent given off by Snow. His man scent was mixed with wolf scent. Since he'd just turned back from werewolf form, I assumed that was the reason.

"I stink," he said with shame. "Don't come too close."

"You don't stink," I assured him. Then, with a mischievous grin, I placed my hand on his solid chest and added, "To tell the truth, you smell rather good. Sexy, in fact."

His entire demeanor relaxed at my teasing and a broad smile consumed his handsome face. My heart swelled with an emotion that, at the time, I didn't recognize since I'd never felt it before. I later realized that it was love. I'd basically fallen in love with Noah at first sight.

"Sexy, huh?" he said with a chuckle. "Maybe we should bottle the scent."

"Maybe you should," I said with a nod as I lightly touched his wounded neck. "Is this the only place you're hurt?"

"I have a gash on my back," he admitted, "but, don't worry. We heal fast."

"Well, if you don't mind, I will worry," I said with a flair of domestic authority. "We happen to have a vet on the premises and I think she should
take a look at you."

He threw his head back in laughter.

"A vet," he roared. "Now, that's rich."

"What are you two cackling about?" Kenzie grumbled as she sat up on the edge of the futon and rubbed the sleep from her eyes. "I heard the word vet amidst laughing."

"Noah has a wicked gash on his neck and he says another on his back," I explained. "I thought he should have you look at them."

"I told her that there is no need," he interjected. "We heal quickly."

"Even so," I said. "I'd feel better if you check him out."

"Is Oscar wounded too?" she asked with concern.

"He gave as good as he got," Noah replied. "Actually, better, since we're alive and they're not."

"That's not an answer," she grumbled.

"I'm good," Oscar merrily chimed as he bounced down the stairwell, sloshing coffee from the two mugs he carried on the way.

"You'd never survive as a server in a restaurant," Kenzie chuckled as she accepted what was left of the steaming mug of coffee that he held out to her.

"Yes, well, it's not my thing, baby," he said with a teasing grin. Pounding his fists against his chest, he added, "Fighting off those who wish to do my woman harm, on the other hand, is."

"Your woman...Spare me," Kenzie said with a mock groan that was mixed with a light laugh.

"You didn't get injured, then?" I asked as I visually searched his neck for a wound that was similar to Noah's.

"Oh, I didn't say that," he replied as he lifted his shirt to expose a gash across his stomach that made Noah's wound on his neck look like a light scratch.

"And you're playfully delivering coffee!" Kenzie screeched. "Get that shirt off and let me look at that!"

"I already took care of both of us," Oscar assured her. "Did you forget that I am also a vet?"

I stared at him as if he'd just told me that he had two heads. I actually had forgotten that he was also a trained medical person. Be it animal or human, he was certainly just as qualified to tend to their wounds as was Kenzie.

He looked at me and grinned, "Ah. You did."

Feeling embarrassed, I quickly asked, "If you tended to them, why aren't they covered."

"He cleaned them of residue from our opponents," Noah explained. "There's no sense in covering them. In a few hours, they'll be gone."

"Seriously?" Kenzie incredulously asked.

"Wait and see," Oscar said with a grin.

19

True to their claim, the brothers' wounds were barely visible by mid-morning. Oscar explained that, had he not tended to them with a special cleaning liquid that their grandfather concocted, their wounds would not have healed so readily and would have left scars. As it was, their bodies were fairly devoid of marks that would mar their beauty.

I kept it to myself that, had Noah been scarred, I would have loved him just the same because my brief moment of intimacy with him was just that. Brief. Just as he'd held me close in his bed while sleeping, only to keep a good distance from me in my waking hours, his intimate demeanor disappeared as soon as we returned to the main floor of the house and he was reminded of the danger that I was in.

His shifting of behavior around me made me question his true reasoning for caring for me. Was it the same love that I felt? Or, was it guilt over the fact that he'd inadvertently exposed me to the world of werewolfism? His aloof and serious behavior made me think that it was the latter.

Leave it to me to finally fall in love with a man only to have him not love me back, I thought as I listened to Noah and Oscar discuss what to do to protect us that night.

"It's not just Lisa who needs protection," Oscar emphasized. "Kenzie may not have the gene, but she's a beautiful woman who they'd readily grab to make more half-breeds."

"Gee, that makes me feel so special," Kenzie sarcastically said.

"It should," Oscar replied. "Only the finest specimens of humanity are accepted into the pack. Because they don't have the gene as strong as a full blooded werewolf, half-breeds require a solid human side to survive the turning each month. Lisa's a watered down half-breed."

"I'm a what?" I screeched.

"You have the gene, but you don't turn," Noah explained. "That tells us that you have the genetics of a human and a werewolf. You are not full werewolf."

"Neither of my parents were werewolves," I protested. "I'd know if they were."

"I'm thinking more your grandparents or great grandparents," he offered. "Had one of your parents been a werewolf, you would turn at the full moon like the rest of us."

"So, half-breeds do everything a full blooded werewolf does?" Kenzie said with open curiosity.

"Yes," Oscar said. "The only difference is that it takes them longer to get used to the shift. The first few shifts are actually excruciatingly painful for a half-breed. A full blooded werewolf doesn't experience pain to that extent. It's still painful in the beginning, but not life threatening."

"What about a watered down one who's been turned?" I asked with concern. "How does that work?"

"The watered down wolf has the gene, but their humanity overpowers it.
The werewolf must be in his full moon form so that when he bites or scratches the watered down wolf, his DNA will activate the gene that's been dormant. It gives it the strength to overcome the humanity genetics during the full moon," Noah explained.

"What about the turning process?" I asked. "If a half-breed suffers during it, what happens to a watered down one?"

"Ouch," Oscar said as he shrugged his shoulders.

"Like the half-breed, it's painful. That pain lasts for a few more full moons than with a half-breed. If done correctly, the werewolf turning the watered down wolf can deposit venom to help the level of genetics and ease the transition a bit. Don't worry.

We won't let you be turned unless you want it," Noah assured me.

"Want it?" I incredulously repeated. "No offence, but why would I want it?"

I could have sworn I saw a glint of disappointment flash across his face before it returned to the stoic expression he was prone to maintain.

"Why do we want most of the things we want?" he said. "It's an individual and personal choice with a reasoning behind it that only you will know or decide upon. No one can or will force it upon you."

The word "good" was on the tip of my tongue, but it never left my mouth. Instead, I said, "When you turn tonight, I'm not going inside. I'm staying right there with you."

20

He could have just been busy, but it seemed to me that Noah spent the rest of the day ignoring me. He was in and out of the house throughout the day, but said minimal to me whenever we were in each other's company. I felt acutely alone. Especially because Kenzie and Oscar took off to do what they could about completing their tagging assignment. Although I still had Snow as my constant companion, our conversations were one sided... me speaking and him listening.

Not only had I been forbidden to go out of the house for fear of being seen, but I was forced to wear that blasted, cumbersome red cape. The only benefit was that when I held it to my nose and sniffed, it hinted of his scent. It gave me a sense of feeling wrapped in his protective arms.

After a few sarcastic jokes about Red Riding Hood, I settled down and gave in to my situation. I had to admit -to myself at least- that I was behaving badly because of the disappointment I felt over unrequited love for Noah. He may not love me, but he clearly felt responsible for me and was doing his best to keep me safe. Pouting like a spoiled child did the situation no good.

"Keeping Snow next to you like that is a good idea. His scent will help to mask yours," Noah said as he offered me a tuna salad sandwich and a snack bag of plain potato chips. Seeing me eye the fare with curiosity, he smiled that handsome smile of his and said, "I picked this up while in town. I hope you
like tuna."

"I do," I said as I gave him a grateful smile and accepted the lunch he was providing. "I can cook, you know. You don't have to order out for me all of the time. I can make a few things."

"That's good to know," he said as he left the room.

Disappointed that I was to eat alone, I sat on the floor and pulled off small pieces of my sandwich to share with Snow. He suspiciously sniffed it before cautiously taking it from me.

"I don't recommend you feed him," Noah said from the doorway.

Not expecting him to return, my body jolted from the surprise and I threw my hand over my heart to help steady it.

"You surprised me," I nervously said.

"He's technically not domestic," he informed me. "Feeding him this kind of food isn't a good idea."

"What do you feed him?" I asked.

"I rarely do," he replied. "He hunts for his food like any other creature in the wild."

"Even when he's with you?" I asked with surprise.

He nodded.

I gave a worried look at Snow as I watched his tongue lick his lips clean.

"I didn't mean any harm," I said.

"The little bit you gave him isn't a big deal, but I wouldn't get him used to it," Noah said. "I'm here for a few hours. Let's give Snow a break and let him do a bit of hunting."

When I nodded, he called for Snow to follow him out of the house. I went to the window and watched as he crouched down to speak into the wolf's ear. Whatever it was that he said was enough to spur the wolf into action. His powerful legs pushed him forward into an impressive speed as he headed for the tree line. Within a matter of seconds, he'd blended with the wild.

Noah remained outdoors for the length of time that it took for me to finish the lunch he'd provided. I was just washing down the last of the chips with a glass of spring water when he returned.

"I need to catch a few winks in preparation

for my second turn tonight," he explained.

Remembering that he'd been up for over twenty-four hours, I sympathetically said, "You must be exhausted."

He shook his head.

"During the full moon we have extra energy," he said. "We require sleep, but not as much. A short nap should do the trick." After a moment of thought, he added, "I hate to do this, but with Snow gone, I'll need you to join me so that I can protect you."

"In bed?" I asked with dismay.

"It's not like we haven't shared a bed before," he matter-of-factly said.

I thought for a moment over what to do. It was true that he'd slept next to me for the first few nights, but, then, I hadn't realized that I'd fallen in love with him. Lying next to him with that knowledge in the forefront while knowing that he didn't feel the same way was sure to be excruciating. Yet, I could see no way out of it. Snow was off hunting and he needed rest.

I reluctantly nodded my head as I made a gesture for him to lead the way to the bedroom.

"You act as if I'm leading you to your doom," he grumbled. "I'm sorry if you find lying next to me that repulsive."

I sucked in air with surprise over his remark.

"I – I don't," I stammered, but said no more.

He removed his shirt and shoes, but kept his jeans on before settling onto the mattress and stretching his arm out to indicate that I should join him. I cautiously curled up into the crook of his arm. A myriad of emotions flooded me. Tears of regret over the fact that he didn't want me the way that I wanted him welled up in my eyes. A lone tear managed to escape before I got my emotions under control.

"I can call Snow back if it's that difficult for you," he murmured.

"It's not," I stammered. "I'm just... it's the tension of anticipation for what might happen tonight."

It wasn't a total lie. I'd just omitted the part about my sadness over unrequited love.

He tightened his arm around me in a protective manner.

"I promise you'll be safe," he said.

I nodded, but remained silent as I listened to his steady heartbeat as it matched the rhythm of his breathing. Little by little my body relaxed as I
joined him in a rejuvenating slumber.

21

The muffled sounds of voices coming from the main room of the house slowly roused me from my slumber. I reached for Noah, but his side of the mattress was empty and cold.

Taking a few minutes to gather my wits about me, I swung my legs to the side of the bed and then padded my way to the ensuite bathroom. After inserting the last of the medication that Dr. Blake provided, I closed my eyes so that I could concentrate on assessing the condition of my body. I felt pretty good. All that remained was a mild soreness in my ribcage which I expected that a few more days would see an end to. During my examination, the doctor declared that there was only a hairline fracture in my rib and that it should heal quickly. Considering the loud crack that I'd heard when that beast fell upon me, I'd experienced doubts about the validity of that claim. I was happy to discover that he was right.

Feeling refreshed and encouraged, I

hurried out to the main room. The sound of an unfamiliar female voice greeted me as soon as I left the bedroom.

I stopped in my tracks as a jealous female voice screeched, "You had her sleeping in your bed?"

"I needed to keep her close," Noah patiently explained. "I had to catch a few winks before tonight."

"You could have called me earlier," the female accusingly said.

"Danica, don't be that way. You know that nothing happened," Noah
said in a way that sounded like it was intended to diffuse her jealousy. "I should have called you, but I didn't think of it until I awoke. Between disposing of bodies, maintaining my work schedule, dealing with pack issues, the full moon, and protecting her, it's been a rough few days. Thankfully, I had Oscar with me.... Who also didn't think to call you, by the way."

"Poor Noah," Danica said in a manner that I couldn't tell whether it was sarcastic or soothing. "You do have a plate full, don't you?"

"Yes, I do," he firmly stated.

Not knowing what to do, I continued entering the room. The woman standing opposite Noah was tall and lean. I guessed her to be at least three inches taller than me. She possessed a sculpted, muscled body that looked like that of a swimmer or a runner. The difference being that most of the runners and swimmers that I'd seen had small breasts and hers were decent in size and well formed. Her dark brown eyes were in stark contrast to the almost platinum hair that flowed down her back to her lumbar region. She had to be the most beautiful creature I'd ever seen.

As I entered the room, this gorgeous blonde turned to glower at me. Even though I was aware of her being there and had actually had the advantage of seeing her before she saw me, I was taken aback for a brief second by the fierceness of her eyes as she looked me over from head to toe.

Having been born with a natural beauty that many women coveted, I was used to their jealousy and insecurity. In my opinion, there was nothing outstanding or exotic about my beauty. I had straight dark hair, a petite and slender body, blue eyes, and pale skin. It hardly rivaled what she possessed. I couldn't understand why this one would be jealous of me, but she clearly was.

I'd grown tired of being timid and afraid. It seemed to be all that I'd felt since my attack. It was understandable in reference to being kidnapped by werewolves, but certainly not because a woman was jealous of my beauty. Instead of cowering, I squared my shoulders and sauntered into the room with as much of a confident façade as I could muster.

"Hello," I said while holding my head high. Ignoring Noah, I directed my attention to Danica. "I'm Lisa."

"I know," she said as she slid close to Noah and placed her arm around his waist. I detected a glint of mischievousness in her eyes as she added, "I understand my honey here has been protecting you from the big bad wolves."

I did my best to hide my disappointment over discovering that they were a couple. Smiling as sweetly as I could manage and still avoiding looking at Noah, I nodded and said, "Both he and Oscar have been helping Snow keep me safe."

The mention of Snow caused her eyes to narrow.

"You've met Snow?" she said with an accusing tone.

I don't know why it gave me so much satisfaction to realize that she was annoyed by that fact, but it did. I'd never been jealous of a woman before. Then, I'd never felt such a powerful pull and connection for a person like I did for Noah before either. It was probably my own female claws coming out because she'd managed to capture the heart of the man who'd captured mine. Whatever the reason, I naughtily capitalized on her animosity.

"Snow saved my life at the lake and has been my constant companion since," I said with hidden delight.

She looked accusingly at Noah.

"You haven't told all to me, honey," she said with false syrupy sweetness. "Snow only protects female werewolves."

I finally allowed myself to look at Noah. He was clearly uncomfortable as he admitted to Danica that I possessed the dormant werewolf gene.

"I thought you said that she was just someone who the Baxter pack coveted," she accused.

"She is. She and her friend Kenzie have both been targeted," he assured her.

"Is this Kenzie also a half-breed?" she asked.

"I'm not a half-breed," I corrected her. "I guess I'm what you'd call watered down."

"You sound like you're proud of this fact," she snipped.

"Should I be ashamed?" I asked with surprised.

The tall beauty left Noah's side. Slowly circling me, she openly scrutinized my body from head to toe.

"You're in werewolf country, my dear," she sneered. "We don't much cotton to humans."

Since I had no desire to be a werewolf

and didn't covet the fact that I carried the gene, I have no idea why I corrected her by saying, "I'm not just a human. I'm a watered down werewolf."

"We value purity around here. Tainted genetics are nothing to be proud of. You're closer to human than to werewolf," she declared. She turned to Noah and said with obvious disapproval, "Have you any idea what the pack will think when they discover that their leader has been sheltering a mutt?"

"Leader?" I said with surprise while ignoring the insult of being called a mutt.

"He didn't tell you?" she said as she turned to me and smiled with smug satisfaction over knowing something that I didn't. "He's our pack leader. Oscar is his second."

I slowly shook my head as I looked at Noah with new eyes. "I didn't know."

"He's pure werewolf, honey," she said with satisfaction. "As am I. The leader of the pack can only mate with a pure werewolf if he wants to keep his position."

"Oscar doesn't plan on it," I contested without thinking.

Danica raised a brow. After a moment of silence, she incredulously asked, "With you?"

I took great satisfaction over the outraged look that overcame her when I informed her that it wasn't me who Oscar loved, but my pure human friend, Kenzie.

22

"Well, well," Oscar bellowed as he and Kenzie entered the room. "I see you called in the troops, brother. William and Joseph are keeping guard outside. They said that they saw signs of Snow's hunting. I was wondering when you were going to send him off to tend to his needs." Turning to Danica, his jovial attitude went sour as he said, "Hello, pain in my ass."

"Hello, shit face," she replied with what I can only describe as an evil sneer.

Kenzie and I simultaneously looked from Danica to Oscar. Their tone of voice and expressions hinted of an interesting story. Curious, but knowing better than to question anyone about their unusual greeting just then, Kenzie stepped forward.

"I'm Kenzie," my friend said as she offered her hand to Danica.

"The human," Danica grumbled as she rejected Kenzie's hand and walked into the kitchen without a backward glance.

Wearing a scowl that was so deep that

it actually marred his handsome face, Oscar turned to his brother and asked, "Why is she here?"

"I didn't know what else to do," Noah replied. "She's been incessantly calling."

"You could change your phone number, for one," he grumbled. After a smug chuckle from his brother, Oscar continued with, "Why don't you just kick her to the curb? You're never going to make her your mate. Don't you think
it's time she got the memo?"

"You're not a couple?" I said to Noah with a bit more exposed enthusiasm than I'd intended.

"She wants it, but they're only bed buddies, and that's all it will ever be," Oscar said with extreme emphasis and loud enough for Danica to hear as he turned to look at me. It was at that moment that a look of horror came over him when he realized what he'd just announced.

"Thanks," Noah scolded as he grabbed his brother by his elbow and escorted him out of the house.

Kenzie and I stifled our humor as we listened to Noah chastise Oscar over his big mouth and loose tongue.

They'd settled down and switched to a new topic that I could only make out as planning for the night with the other two werewolf men when Danica returned.

"You're still here?" she huffed as she stomped passed me. "Take a hint and pack your bags. We'd all be the better for it."

"You're just a barrel of polite sunshine," Kenzie snipped as she sat down in the nearest chair and made herself comfortable. When Danica gave her that evil glower that she'd only recently blessed me with, my friend's chin lifted high as she said, "Don't think you can intimidate me. I've seen sad cases like you before. Beautiful on the outside but ugly on the inside. You have to cling to the man by offering him your pooty-tang in hopes it will be enough to snare him into something more permanent since your winning personality doesn't cut it. Trust me when I say this. Werewolf or human... if he can get the milk without buying the cow, he's gonna keep doing it until a new and more challenging cow comes along. Maybe even for a while afterward since the new cow knows better than to put out like some desperate whore."

An ear piercing scream that sounded like it was blended with a deep growl came from somewhere in Danica's throat as she lept onto Kenzie with her fingernails in position to do the most harm. My eyes went wide as I watched her fingers elongate along with her nails until they looked more like animal claws than human hands.

"Kenzie, watch out!" I bellowed in

reaction to the sight of what was happening.

Of course, my crying out a warning came far too late. Her body had already disappeared beneath Danica's by that time. I was about to grab a small statue from a nearby table to club the vicious she-wolf over the head with when there was a turn of events. Kenzie's years of wrestling with livestock and large domestic animals while tending to them had made her not only strong, but clever in the take-down. Before my very eyes, she had Danica flat on her back on the floor beneath her. The hatred and rage on the she-wolf's face could be seen beneath the mass of flaxen hair that fell wildly across it.

She was sitting astride her attacker while pinning Danica's formidable claw-like hands against the floor when the men flew in to investigate the raucous.

"Tell me what to do, Oscar," Kenzie panted with a rage that I'd never seen in her. "Should I cut off her head? From what I've seen of the little bitch, we'd be all the better for it."

"Shit! Kenz!" Oscar bellowed as he stood at Danica's head and looked down with a panic. "What the hell? What happened?"

"Lisa! Get me a kitchen knife so we can be rid of this abomination!" Kenzie bellowed. When I didn't move, she shouted, "Now, Lisa!"

With the exception of Oscar standing at Danica's head, not one of the men made an effort to intervene. I looked at Noah to find that his face was pale and he wore an expression of concern, but he stayed motionless.

"Noah?" I said with surprise. "What's happening? Stop this." When he still made no move to intervene, I knelt on the floor next to my irate friend and gently placed my hand on her shoulder. "Kenzie, stop. Please. You're better than this."

I kept my hand firmly placed on her shoulder while gently coaxing her to stop until the crazy look in my friend's eyes slowly faded back to normal. When she jumped off Danica, I lost my balance and fell onto my backside. Ignoring my situation, she stormed out of the house without giving any of us a second glance.

Instead of thanking me for being the only one to intervene, Danica turned to look at me with eyes of hate. Had I not already been on the floor, her look would have surely knocked me onto it.

I watched the she-wolf pick herself up with as much dignity as possible and then stand in front of Noah with her head bent low. He picked up one of her altered hands and inspected Kenzie's blood beneath her nails.

"You were foolish, Danica," he scolded.

"She had every right to behead you." Dropping her hand as if it was an item that disgusted him, he ordered, "Go clean up and prepare for the turn."

She slithered out of the room without looking at any of the occupants. Oscar moved to me and extended his hand to assist me onto my feet.

"I don't much care for the girl," he whispered into my ear while still holding my hand. "Even so, I would have hated to have Kenzie caught up in the mess that would have surely occurred if a human beheaded her."

"She's that special?" I said with a trembling voice that was filled with the adrenaline that had fueled me to do what the others couldn't or wouldn't do.

"She's the granddaughter of a former pack leader," he explained. "It makes her like royalty. She's not the only one who wants to see her mated with Noah. I'd dare say that most of the pack feels that way."

I looked at Noah, who had his back to us and his head lowered in conversation with the other two men.

"You and Noah don't, though?" I hesitantly said.

"I definitely don't," he replied. "As for my brother... sometimes I just don't know what he thinks."

23

Kenzie and I sat on the front porch while we watched the sun slowly ease its way behind the trees.

"The moon will be full again tonight," she mused. "I reckon we'll see the turning in about four hours."

"How did you know that you had the right to cut off her head?" I asked as I vigorously rocked in the Adirondack styled rocking chair. "No one was going to stop you."

"I know," she said with a sigh. "I sometimes lose it when I'm around bitches like her. It stems from my high school days. I wasn't a beauty, as you well can see, and I was picked on quite a bit by the popular girls."

"I think you're beautiful," I said in earnest. "So does Oscar."

She gave me an affectionate smile.

"I've got a long way to go to be in your category of looks, but I will admit that I've grown into myself," she said. "It's sort of like the ugly duckling becoming a swan. Not a gorgeous swan, mind you, but a swan with some fine attributes all the same."

"I think you short sell yourself," I firmly said. "Anyway, with that aside, how did you know?"

"I've been grilling Oscar on the ways of the werewolf," she admitted. "He wants to take our relationship to the next level and I couldn't say one way or the other without being informed on what I'd be getting in to or out of."

"So, by attacking you, she set herself up for a beheading?" I incredulously asked.

"Not quite," she said. "It was more the fact that she shifted in front of me while attacking that gave me the right to kill her. It's considered self-defense. If she'd killed me, they'd have done nothing about it either."

"What?" I softly exclaimed. "She attacked you and would get away with it?"

"She attacked me with provocation," she said. "I did provoke her, after all."

I giggled as I nodded and said, "Yes, you did."

She threw her head back in laughter.

"I wish we'd filmed the whole thing," she wistfully said. "I would love to be able to go over it all and see her getting her ass beat in slow motion."

"You surprised me," I said. "I was just

about to club her over the head with that little statue on the table near the television when you got the better of her. Remind me not to piss you off."

"You never could," she reassured me. "You're beautiful, true, but your beauty runs deep. That creature's beauty stopped at her skin. Inside, she's ugly as sin and evil at heart. You're nothing like her."

"Yet, Noah ignores me," I pouted.

"He's wrestling with himself," Kenzie said. "Don't tell anyone I told you this, but Oscar said that he's fighting his attraction to you because you're not pure werewolf. Apparently, his pack expects him to mate with a pure werewolf.
Archaic, right?"

"Danica was quick to tell me that fact," I said with a sigh. "But her? Is he really considering her?"

"Apparently, pure werewolves are a rarity. It's not like he has a lot to choose from and, from what I understand, they're already sleeping together," she said with a shrug. "I think it's a shame. You two would make a kick ass couple if I do say so."

"Why am I suddenly sorry that I'm not a werewolf?" I said with surprise. "Is that crazy?"

"Love can make you crazy," she said.

"I do, you know," I said in a low voice so that only she could hear me as I stopped rocking and looked directly at her. "I've never loved before. Leave it to me to finally fall in love and have it be with someone who can't or won't allow himself to love me back."

"It's a damn shame," she said with a slow shake of the head. "I've experienced unrequited love. I feel for you, my friend."

I heaved a sigh and squared my shoulders. There was nothing to do but to get over it and move on.

"When can we go home?" I asked. "Is it over after tonight?"

Her eyes went wide as she said, "He didn't tell you?"

Suddenly uneasy with dread, I asked, "Tell me what?"

"They're going to keep coming after you until you're mated with one of them," she said. "You can't be left unattended which means you can't go home."

"Ever?" I practically screeched with dismay.

She shook her head and said with a sad tone, "Not until you have a mate. I'm so very sorry."

"Just me?" I said as I remembered that she was also a target.

She looked down and smiled, "I'm technically mated. I've agreed to marry Oscar."

"Marry?" I half asked, half exclaimed.

149

When she blushed and gave a broad smile, I lept from my chair to hug her. Since she was still sitting down, it was an awkward hug, at best, but she got the emotion behind it just fine.

"You don't have the gene," I suddenly remembered. "How will that work."

"We'll live like any other man and wife. The difference being that he'll leave me during the full moon to join his pack," she explained.

"What do I do?" I asked as the realization struck me that I was doomed to a lifetime of being chased by werewolves.

"That's a dilemma," she said. "If only Noah wasn't so stuck on tradition. I'm hoping we can change his mind. If not, we'll have to introduce you to another werewolf who isn't so stuck on purity of genetics."

"I don't think he's as stuck on purity as he is on the desires of his pack," I said.

"Leave it to you to defend him," she chuckled. "If he only knew what a gem he was passing on."

24

I was both disgusted and frustrated.

A week earlier I had no idea that werewolves existed anywhere but in fairy tales, books, and movies. Suddenly, not only were they real, but they existed below our social radar in a world of their own with rules of their own. By some sick twist of fate, I'd fallen into this underground reality and was forced to deal with the fact that I'd never be free of it.

If I wanted some semblance of normality to return, I had no other option than to give in and find someone to mate with. Then, I'd be able to go home and resume a life of writing books and enjoying small town living.

Sadly, the thought of committing myself to a man simply to be able to lead a normal life was overwhelmingly oppressive. This was especially hard hitting because the man wouldn't be Noah.

I longed for the same joy that my

friend Kenzie was experiencing. Hers came from years of devoted friendship that eventually became love. I couldn't expect such a blessing for myself. I'd never felt the emotions that I experienced whenever I was near Noah before I met him and I doubted I'd feel them again with anyone else.

I'd repeatedly told myself that it was impossible to fall in love with a man so quickly. I'd read that it happened and had met a few people who claimed to have experienced love at first sight, but I never really put much stock in it. I didn't recognize what I felt for him as love right away, but it came to light within a few days which was quick in my book. The only way that I could explain it was that it was a rare connecting of pheromones that happened to a select few.

What I found to be most infuriating was that I could feel the attraction that he had for me whenever he was near. He may not have felt for me in the same way and capacity that I did him, but he was definitely drawn to me.

I was so frustrated and angry with him for the fact that his devotion to his pack and his principles would prevent him from following his heart that, had he been in front of me just then, I'd have wrung his neck.

I was sitting on the front porch waiting for the moon to rise to its fullest when Noah joined me.

"You'd better go inside now," he said with a soft, but authoritative tone.

Defiantly lifting my chin, I asked, "Why?"

"It's not safe for you out here," he grumbled. "Oscar and I are the only ones who are truly concerned for your welfare. The only reason the others are keeping a distance is because of my position. I don't trust Danica not to start something once they've turned."

"They'd attack me after they shifted even though I'm under the protection of their pack master?" I said with disbelief. "What does that say for their respect for you and your position?"

I knew that I was being obnoxious and ungrateful, but I couldn't help myself. Since the feelings I had for him were new for me, I wasn't dealing with them very well. I was hurt that he didn't want me enough to fight for me, so I wanted to hurt him back the only way I knew how.

He heaved a sigh while he focused on keeping a stoic facade.

"It would make life a lot easier for me if you and Snow would return to the basement," he said. "Please."

I glowered at him long enough for me to call him several unflattering names in my head for not wanting me like I wanted him.

"Well, let's not make life difficult for *you*," I spat before stomping off into the house to find Snow.

"I'm coming with you," Kenzie said as she pulled herself free from Oscar's loving embrace.

The sight of their overly affectionate behavior was like razor blades across my emotions. I quickly called for Snow and scurried down into the basement before anyone could witness the tears flowing down my cheeks.

Hot on my heels, Kenzie hurriedly scooped me into her arms. Pouring my heart out to my friend, I explained how difficult I found dealing with these new emotions was.

"It makes me not want to continue living, I just can't imagine what life is going to be like now. My world was perfect before this. Perfect," I complained. "I regret the day I ever set eyes on Noah Spears.

"I have to say that I regret it too," my dear friend said. "Not just because of the way you feel about Noah, but because your life is changed forever and it's because of me. If I hadn't insisted on bringing you along to the cabin, you
wouldn't be in this pickle."

"I don't blame you," I sniffed. "I don't blame anyone. It was probably my fate to have my genetic heritage come to the surface at some point. I just wish that I'd met the man of my dreams along with learning about it. I can't stay under Noah and Oscar's protection forever. I'll have to settle for a relationship with someone who I don't feel connected to. I've been there before and it wasn't pleasant."

"Maybe we can mate you with someone who won't really want to live with you," Kenzie hopefully suggested.

"Just how would that work?" I asked. "From what I can tell, this mating thing is more for procreation than anything else. The guy would want to sleep with me."

"You've slept with men that you haven't loved before," she protested. "If Noah is your first true love, then all the others were simply men you liked. I'm sure we can find a werewolf man who you can like at least as much as you've liked your past boyfriends. Maybe more. It won't be such an intolerable situation. I promise."

"I suppose it could work," I said with a sigh. "It's just that after escaping a marriage that would have oppressed me for the rest of my life, I'd thought to put off considering it again for at least another five years or so. I was enjoying my freedom after living under Rob's domination. I don't want to be dominated and controlled like that again. Do I have to marry him under the eyes of our human law? I mean, are the children even registered? I can't imagine they are if Noah and Oscar are disposing of headless bodies without concern of getting caught."

"I'll be sure to have Oscar investigate your intended to make sure he's not overbearing. As for the children, you're right," she said. "I don't know how they manage it, but, the births are not registered. As far as the government is concerned, these wolf people don't exist."

"I have a lot to learn about this world within our world," I mused.

She gave a broad smile as she said, "That's an excellent way to put it."

The sound of wolves howling outside the house caught our attention. It created a far more sinister atmosphere than the night before when just Noah and Oscar shifted in the moonlight. Danica had made sure that the entire pack gathered in the clearing behind the house for the shifting.

Peering out from behind the blinds of the sliding glass door, I watched Danica make her transition from a beautiful female to an equally beautiful wolf. Snow crept up beside me. I could see and feel the exchange of looks between him and Noah's she-wolf bed buddy. His long, threatening growl told me all that I needed to know about what he thought of the little wolf princess.

25

The pack's howling faded into the distance, but there was still an odd, almost creepy feel in the air. I mentioned it to Kenzie and she readily agreed.

"I don't know if they'll be coming back like they did last night," she nervously said. "Oscar hinted about the need to keep Danica busy so that she couldn't circle back and cause us harm."

"That's just dandy," I hissed. "What if someone from another pack shows up like they did last night? What do we do then?"

"I asked him that very same question," she admitted.

"And?" I said and then waited with eager silence to hear his solution.

She shrugged as she informed me that Noah was posting his most loyal men around the perimeter of the land to keep watch for invaders.

"Will that be enough?" I asked. "What if someone slips past them? After all, from what I hear, we aren't all that big a priority for them."

She scowled while slowly shaking her head.

"I think we should come up with a plan in case that happens," she said with a determined voice. "I'd rather be prepared and have nothing happen than have to do last minute survival thinking."

"Survival?" I gasped. "I thought they wanted us for mates. Would they actually kill us?"

"I don't know," she moaned. "After seeing the jealousy that Danica had for both of us and knowing that female mates are at a premium, I don't trust that the few females they have wouldn't contrive a way to get rid of us."

"You'd think just the opposite," I mused. "You'd think that they'd appreciate the company."

"Maybe if we were pure blooded," she offered, "but you're watered down and I haven't a hint of their gene to my possession. You heard the wolf princess. As far as they're concerned, we're an insult and an abomination."

"Wolf princess," I chuckled. "If that's royalty, I'm glad I'm common."

"Noah and Oscar are also royalty," she mused. "Isn't that funny?"

"Yes. Very funny," I replied as I stroked Snow's head between his ears.

He surprised me by showing far more affection than one might expect from a creature of the wild.

"Did he just kiss your face?" Kenzie asked with surprise. When I nodded and wiped at the saliva that he'd left behind, she said, "That's so unusual."

"Why?" I asked. "Dogs do it all of the time."

"Dogs are domesticated," she reminded me. "Snow is not. Oscar told me that Noah takes great pains to make sure of that. If that wolf is kissing you, it means something. I just don't know what."

"I can tell you exactly what it means," came a discarnate male voice that hinted of a Scottish brogue from the far side of the room.

To my surprise, Snow did not react in a negative way to the voice. Instead, he trotted in the direction that it came from and stood as if patiently waiting for someone or something.

"Who's that?" Kenzie said in a hushed whisper as she nervously grabbed a poker from the nearby fireplace and took a defensive position.

"I can't see anyone," I said as I frantically looked for something to grab as well.

Finding nothing nearly as lethal as what Kenzie managed to obtain, I picked up a heavy glass bowl and readied it to hit whoever belonged to that voice in the head if he came any closer.

"Show yourself," Kenzie ordered with a tremble that failed to belie her nervousness.

"I can show myself to Lisa, but, alas, Kenzie, you do nay have the capacity to see me," the voice said. "You must have the gift, as I am deceased."

"A ghost!" she exclaimed.

"Hello, Snow," the voice said in a gentle manner. "How are ya, old boy?"

I found it amazing that the wolf showed his delight in hearing the voice with both body language and vocalizing. It made me wonder if he was able to see its owner as well.

I couldn't just see ghosts out of the blue. It required that I shifted my energy frequency. I found it taxing on my body and tiring, so I rarely did it. When I did, I didn't do it for long periods of time.

As if reading my thoughts, the voice said, "Do nay fret, Lisa. I will be short in explaining things to you. You should nay be taxed by the session." After a moment of silence and my still debating about whether I should shift my energy frequency to see the spirit, he added, "If you desire, I can simply speak without being seen. Snow sees me without effort. That is good enough for me."

Although I'd seen and spoken to spirits

on multiple occasions, it had always been on my terms. I called them in and ran the show. Having one appear like this with such a strong connection to my side of the reality veil was a little disconcerting. Because he had so much clarity of voice and I could literally see Snow's fur moving where he must have been petting him, I doubted I'd have to do much frequency shifting. Even so, I was uncomfortable with the whole thing and decided that seeing him wasn't all that important.

"Since I need to conserve my strength in the event that something might go down tonight, I think I'll pass on seeing you, if you don't mind," I said with soft timidity.

"Really?" Kenzie said with surprise. "If I had the ability to see who was attached to that voice, I'd definitely want to do it."

I vigorously shook my head.

"It could potentially sap me of all my strength with hours of recovery," I informed her.

Heaving a sigh, she looked to where Snow sat and said, "Okay, then. Speak."

"You can put that poker down, young lady," the voice said with humor. "It will do no good for you in this situation."

As Kenzie returned the poker to its rightful place and I set the bowl back on the side table, he suggested that we sit and get comfortable.

Even though Snow seemed actually happy to have this unseen visitor, I remained suspicious. Therefore, I selected the chair that would keep me furthest from the voice.

"Allow me to introduce myself," the voice said. "I am Logan McKean. Your great, great, great, great grandfather."

Although I knew of his existence, I'd been told very little about an ancestor named Logan McKean. All I knew was that he was a warrior and a chief of some tribe back in the day. Even so, hearing him declare himself to me felt right. So, I said nothing and just listened to what he had to say.

"Noah is a fool," Logan began, "as is Oscar. Neither of them have the sense to question and research what it is that they feel coming from you, Lisa. It is nay watered down genetics. It is royal genetics of an old line."

"How can that be?" I asked with concern. "These werewolf people seem too proud of their heritage not to keep track. Wouldn't I have been told by my ancestors if I was royal?"

"Normally, aye," he said, "but this is a case where your genetics were kept secret and the turning cycles bound by a very powerful magician." When I gave Kenzie a look of disbelief, he continued with, "Let me start from the beginning. I was head of a very respected family of werewolves in the

highlands. It was a time of wonder. A time of magic. Today, modern technology interferes with nature and prohibits the use of the earth's natural magic, but, in my time, those who were skilled in its use could perform
wonderous feats."

I sucked in air as his words struck a chord within me that validated their truth.

"During this time, vampires were prevalent in Europe. More so there, than anywhere else. As I am sure you have learned from stories of old, vampires and werewolves are mortal enemies," he said. "It was the design of the evil one who created us. I ken it was done for his amusement."

I gave Kenzie a bewildered look as I said in a hushed tone, "Vampires are real too?"

Looking just as aghast at the idea, she shrugged and said, "I don't know, but I can't argue against it either."

"Arguing against their existence will nay make them go away," Logan lightly scolded. "What did help to separate them from mankind to the extent that they are now less of a threat than the werewolf was magic. You see, the war between the vampire nest and my pack became so severe and gruesome that we were at risk of becoming extinct. My council and I held a meeting to discuss our situation. We determined that, if we continued to war against our enemies in such a way, there was no telling if any of us would have survived. I was nay willing to take that chance. Nor was the council."

"So, the vampires killed off the werewolves?" I asked.

"As did the werewolves kill off the vampires," he explained. "Numbers on both sides dwindled until I finally made an agreement with the vampire leader.
We agreed to bind our werewolfism if they would bind their vampirism."

"Vampires live on blood," I said with curiosity. "At least, that's the way it is in the stories. How can they bind that?"

"They turned to drinking the blood of animals instead of humans," he said. "They also drank from a chalice instead of piercing the flesh with their teeth. You will find this tradition was common practice amongst pagans. Since they took to drinking their blood in this fashion, their fangs became obsolete and eventually disappeared. Today, you can nay tell them apart from a human."

"So, there really are modern day vampires," Kenzie mused with mild wonderment.

"Indeed there are, lass," he replied. "There are also age old vampires, although the few that exist stay in an alternate realm and rarely cross into yours. If only the unbound werewolves would do the same."

"What happened to our pack?" I asked.

"Ah," he said with enthusiasm. "I was getting to that next. With our werewolfism bound, we stopped turning at the full moon. The difference between us and the vampire is that we did not alter. We are simply bound. The children of my children all have the gene in them. It never has been what they refer to as watered down. None of your ancestors are human. They are all bound werewolves. The details of our binding and heritage stopped being passed from generation to generation out of necessity for secrecy. We found it much easier for our children to live amongst humans if they were ignorant of their true makeup. Even so, the selection of mates has remained discerning to prevent this watering down that the werewolves speak of from happening to our line."

"Are you saying that my parents' marriage was arranged?" I asked.

"Your ancestors on this side of the veil determined that your parents should meet, knowing that they would take to each other. We shifted energies and spoke in their ear to make it happen. If you wish to call that an arranged marriage, then, aye," he said. "I will testify that they loved each other deeply. That is something that must come naturally. We can nay make love happen. It springs forth from a good match." After a short chuckle, he said, "We take pride in our matchmaking."

Hearing this bit of information gave me food for thought. If he was able to make it so that my parents would meet and fall in love, perhaps he was behind my meeting Noah as well.

"Did you arrange for me to meet Noah?" I eagerly asked.

"Alas, that was nay what was intended," he said with a sad voice. "Although, he is pure werewolf and of royal lineage, Noah's pack comes from the line of our adversaries."

"Adversaries? Don't werewolves stick together?" I said with surprise.

"Just like not all of the vampires allowed themselves to be bound, not all of the werewolves supported my decision to bind my pack with magic," he explained. "Noah is from the line that resented it the most. They considered us an abomination and vowed to destroy us. So, instead of having the vampires as our enemy, we had our own kind trying to kill us. It is because of packs like Noah's that we were forced to stop handing down the history of our family to our children. If you did nay know that you were of werewolf lineage, you stood a more favorable chance of living a good life among the humans without strife and danger.

"Are you telling me that if Noah or Oscar find out that I come from the McKean pack, they'll kill me?" I asked with concern.

"Your last name is nay McKean, correct?" he asked.

"It's Keen," I replied.

"Aye," he said. "The name was changed to throw them off. That was good thinking."

"You didn't answer me," I grumbled.

"I nay ken what they might do," he said with a sad tone. "It has been generations since our pack was bound and gone into hiding among the humans. The hatred for us has been passed down, but I am not sure how much of it Noah or Oscar have absorbed. I have been watching them. They seem level-headed and kind. As for certain members of his pack or those who he associates with from other packs, I can tell you here and now that, if they are given the opportunity, they will nay hesitate to kill you."

I looked at Kenzie and asked with a hint of panic in my voice, "What do I do?"

"It is nay just you who they will nay accept, lass," he continued. "I fear for you as well, Kenzie. "It is nay unheard of for a werewolf to mate with a human, but this pack does nay abide it. Oscar must realize this."

"He said that he'll leave the pack if they

don't accept me," she confessed.

His tone was low and saddened as he said, "That is much easier said than done, lass. We can only hope that along with the passing of time, their strict beliefs and traditions have altered in your favor."

26

Because I passed on shifting my energy frequency to see him, I was able to engage in conversation with my great, great, great grandfather for the majority of the evening. With Kenzie just as interested in learning about my ancestry as I was, the time was filled with questions as it passed without us feeling it.

We saw no sign of Noah, Oscar, or any of the pack. Logan checked with the people on his side of the veil and was told that a few of Noah's most trustworthy pack members were standing watch on the perimeter. The rest of the pack was far off on the other side of the mountain hunting.

A way to divert Danica's attention, no doubt.

With only a few hours left before the moon and the sun traded places, Kenzie and I were feeling pretty relaxed and content. Because of this, it took a moment for the sound of someone walking about upstairs to register with us.

Kenzie's eyes went wide when it suddenly struck her that the house had been invaded.

"There's someone here," she urgently whispered.

"I fear he is nay aligned with Noah's pack," Logan lamented.

"We spent all this time talking instead of making plans on what to do if this happened," I bitterly bemoaned.

"I am sorry, lass," he said with a fading voice. "Causing you harm was nay my intent."

I could tell that he was leaving us, but I had no time to worry about it or even say goodbye.

I frantically looked around for something to defend myself with. When my eyes settled on the poker that Kenzie had grabbed at the onset of the night, she touched my arm and silently shook her head. I understood what she meant. There were at least two people upstairs. Our guess was that they were werewolf people searching for us. Knowing the strength they possessed and the fact that there were two of these powerful creatures, it made sense that defending ourselves with one lone poker would be futile.

Pointing to the small door within the paneling, I quickly moved to open it. Pulling her into the cubby with me, I quickly discovered that there was only enough room for one of us to comfortably fit. Two would make it incredibly cramped. Since I suffered from severe claustrophobia, I knew that I'd never survive such an environment for any length of time. I had no desire to take the space away from her, so I quickly exited. There had to be another place for me to hide in. I just needed to be creative and look around.

Kenzie quickly followed me out. I tried to push her back into it, but she vigorously shook her head. We were still battling over who would hide in the little cubby when two large male werewolves came bounding down the stairs.

They were on the cusp of turning back into human form again, so they looked less beastlike than had they come for us a few hours earlier. Because of this, I found them more comical and less scary.

"Well, if you aren't a sight," I jeered with open amusement as they moved toward me.

My outburst caused them to stop in their tracks. As they looked at each other with bewilderment and surprise, I seized the opportunity to grab the fireplace poker and swing it as hard as I could against the closest one's head. Taking my lead, Kenzie moved like the wind to pick up a dog shaped, wrought iron boot scraper that was positioned on the floor near the sliding door. When she threw it as hard as she could at the other one's head, a loud crack permeated the air as it hit its mark.

Without taking the time to see what damage we'd done to our would be abductors, we raced out of the sliding door and across the lawn. We didn't stop until we were deep into the trees.

Winded and running on adrenaline, we took a moment to catch our breath and gather our wits about us.

"So much for the guards along the perimeter," Kenzie hissed.

Pointing to a barely visible figure slumped onto the ground a few yards away, I said, "I think that might be one of them over there."

We cautiously made our way closer to the male who lay in a heap amongst the forest debris. Since he was also in that state of starting to return to human form, I was better able to recognize his features.

"I think this is William," I said as I knelt down next to him.

Kenzie quickly joined me and began checking for vital signs.

"He's alive," she said, "but his breathing is shallow."

I gently cradled his head in my hands and moved it so that I could see its back side. Blood oozed between my fingers as I carefully pulled my hands away.

"He has a pretty big gash on the back of his head," I said with a shudder. "I think his skull might be cracked."

"We need to get him some help," she said with concern. "I wish I knew how badly we injured those two back there. If they're going to pursue us, we're screwed."

"I can go back to see if they're following us," I offered.

She vigorously shook her head.

"Not a good idea," she said. "Not only could they capture you, but I don't think we should separate."

"What do we do?" I asked.

She pursed her lips together.

"Remember this morning when we made a fuss over those gashes that Oscar and Noah got and they simply laughed it off?" she asked. "By midday, they were healed. Maybe he'll heal like that too."

"Or maybe those house invaders will," I pointed out. "Oscar and Noah got those injuries when they were full on werewolves. I wonder if it makes a difference what stage they're in when they get injured."

"I think we need to risk it and leave this man where he lay," she urgently said. "I can hear those two coming."

"Damn! That doesn't sit right with me, but I see your point." I hissed as I stood up and looked around to determine what direction to run. "I have no clue where we are."

"I do," she said as she grabbed my hand and pulled me behind her. "I canvased these woods for lone wolves to tag, remember? There's a cave not far from here that we can hide in. I found it by chance. Hopefully, they won't know about it."

We raced like the wind in the direction of the cave. I was grateful that Kenzie was a seasoned outdoors person who had some sense of where we were and what type of terrain we'd be running over. Considering the moon's light barely filtered through the trees enough to allow good vision, I'd say that she did a bang up job of getting us to the cave with minimal cuts, bruises, or scrapes.

27

It was cold, dark, and dank inside the cave. Neither of us had on adequate coverings for such an environment. We couldn't have been inside it for more than a few minutes before our bodies felt the full impact of the cold.

"I can't stop my teeth from chattering," I complained, "It's like my body has a mind of its own."

"Huddle close to me," she stuttered past teeth that were behaving the same as mine. "If we share our body heat, we might be able to get it under control." After I snuggled into her so close that my only other option would have been to climb beneath her skin, she added, "I didn't realize how damp it was in here. I was properly dressed when I found it."

"Did you come in?" I asked.

"I hid from a bear for about thirty minutes," she replied.

"A bear?" I gasped. "There are bears in these woods?"

"Bears, bobcats, wolves," she said. "Its nature, my dear."

"How did you keep the bear from smelling you?" I asked.

"I had the wolf scent on me," she explained. "For the most part, bears tend to ignore wolves and vice versa."

"Do you think it's still around?" I nervously asked.

"I don't know," she said. "What I do know is that we're in greater danger from those two werewolves who tried to abduct us than we are from that bear."

Just then, a loud crunching of forest floor debris caught our attention. I could feel her body go tense as I held my breath and listened for the direction that the crunching would take. We'd covered the mouth of the cave with brush, but our scent was still prevalent. With any luck, whatever was making that noise wasn't looking for us and would move away without mishap.

Staying as motionless as possible, I cursed my heart for disrupting my hearing with its thunderous pounding. It was almost impossible to see Kenzie in the darkness of the cave, but I could feel her body react to the noise outside as whoever or whatever was making it drew nearer.

The anticipation of whether or not we'd be discovered was excruciating. I was about to question how much longer I'd be able to stand it and not frantically flee when the crunching moved away from the mouth of the cave. I giggled softly from relief as we both simultaneously released the breath we'd been holding.

We waited for what seemed like hours in the cold, damp, darkness, but was only a matter of minutes, to see if whoever or whatever would return. When we heard no more noises, we pushed the brush away from the front of the mouth of the cave to allow us to peer outside.

I heaved a huge sigh of relief when I saw that the sun was peeking over the treetops. It was safe to go back to Noah's house.

"I need to think on what to do next," I said as we carefully made our way back to the house.

"That old ghost gave you some pretty wild information," Kenzie said as she picked up a twig from the ground and played with it while she walked beside me. "Are you going to tell Noah?"

I vigorously shook my head.

"Let's face it," I said. "I barely know him. Now that I understand what lies behind my attraction for him, I don't truly trust how I feel. I thought that it was love. Now, I'm just wondering if it's not just like attracted to like."

"That's not such a bad thing, is it?"

177

she asked.

"Except that it's a one sided attraction," I pouted.

"No, it's not," she insisted. "He was just holding back because he thought that you were watered down, or whatever. Once he learns the truth..."

"He'll either kill me or want me," I interrupted. "If he wants me, then I have to ask myself if I want to be with someone who can be so prejudice."

"Wow. Prejudice? Really?" she said with a raised brow. When I gave her a look that affirmed what I'd just said, she shrugged and said, "Okay. I get it."

We'd reached the clearing when Oscar raced up to us and scooped Kenzie into his arms.

"I was so worried," he said between the kisses that he planted all over her face. "What happened? Where did you go? I thought you'd been taken."

"I guess that means that our would be abductors recovered from the blows to their heads," I said.

"You fought them off?" he said with surprise in his voice.

"You should have seen the swing on Lisa. She cracked one of them over the head with a poker so hard that I could hear it where I stood," Kenzie said with pride. "It spurred me to toss that wrought iron boot scraper at the other one's head. Fortunately, he was so surprised by what Lisa had done to his companion that he froze long enough for my aim to hit its mark."

"Damn, ladies," he said with a grin. "Remind me not to get on your bad side."

I could see Noah standing in the doorway watching us approach. He wore a look of obvious relief. A slight smile formed on my lips. It quickly disappeared when Danica slid up behind him and put her arm around his waist.

I couldn't help wondering what the little wolf princess would do if she knew the truth about me. As tempting as it was to toss it in her face, I knew better. Instead, I nodded to them both as I entered the house and said nothing.

28

Having spent the night awake with my great, great, great, great grandfather's ghost before running for safety from abductors, I was in dire need of sleep. Since it was daylight and Danica was refusing to leave, I was given the guest room with the assurance that I would be guarded at all times. My lucky friend, Kenzie, went off with Oscar. I wasn't sure, but I assumed they went to one of their homes.

"So, even though the full moon is passing, I'm still in danger. Is that what you're saying?" I bitterly asked as I listened to Noah's offering of the guest room. "Is there no end to this nightmare?"

He looked at the floor.

"I wish I could say differently," he replied.

"I can't stay with you forever," I grumbled as I allowed him to escort me into the room. Standing at the door, I turned to look at him which prevented him from entering behind me. "Not only do I have a life of my own, but your future *mate* doesn't care for me much."

A deep frown formed on his handsome face and his eyes grew dark with disapproval.

"Who told you that she was to be my mate?" he asked with angst as he looked over his shoulder in the direction that I knew Danica stood waiting. "It's not true."

I raised a brow and smirked.

"Perhaps you need to inform your little she-wolf of this fact," I said with a hint of sarcasm as I closed the door to the guest room in his face.

I knew that I was being rude and ungrateful, but I couldn't help myself. Whatever it was that I felt when he was near me was an emotion that I had difficulty dealing with. It both frustrated and angered me to be in such a situation. Right or wrong, since it started with him, I took my frustrations out on him.

I visited blissful slumberland for the better part of the day. Since it was my desire to avoid my new life, I could have probably remained there through the night if it wasn't for the overly loud voices coming from the main room.

With my head still groggy and my eyes heavy with sleep, I made my way to the ensuite guest bath. It was smaller than that of the master bathroom, but it contained the same fine quality fixtures. I had to admit that Noah had excellent taste even if his chosen style of decor didn't match mine.

It was my intention to simply wash the sleep from my face at the sink, but, when I set eyes on the gold trimmed, octagon shower that stood in the corner of the room, I decided to give my body a full wash. It would have been a delightful experience after hovering in that cave and tromping through the woods with insufficient clothing had Danica's shrill screaming not penetrated past the pounding water from the showerhead.

"What do you mean she's moving in here?" Danica screeched. "I won't have it, Noah. Do you hear me? I won't have it!"

His voice was much lower and difficult to make out. I could only guess that he was telling her that he didn't care what she would or wouldn't have since she continued to argue the point until I'd finished washing, dried off, gotten dressed, run a comb through my wet hair, and left the guest room.

Placing my hands on my hips, I stood a few yards away from them. When I finally caught their attention, I said with a commanding tone, "Did anyone think to ask me what I wanted?"

Danica made to say something and then stopped in mid-sentence. With her mouth still opened with unsaid words, her eyes narrowed as she looked me up and down.

At first, I thought that she disapproved of the Daisy Duke shorts I'd opted to wear.

Then it struck me.

In my impatience to dress and join them in their lively discussion about my housing, I'd foregone putting on a bra. With my long dark hair still wet, the thin, off-white tee shirt that I'd slipped on did little to disguise my pert nipples that were reacting to the cool wetness that my hair provided.

When I realized her reason for such a hateful stare, my first instinct was to rush back into the guest room and rectify the situation. I was about to do just that when I noticed that Noah was also staring at my breasts. Unlike Danica, his eyes displayed his appreciation for what they saw.

Something devilish surfaced inside of me. Instead of retreating to the guest room, I straightened my spine and squared my shoulders to better display my dark, rosebud nipples that strained against the wet, almost transparent fabric. Not only was I enjoying the fact that it irked Danica beyond reason that my goods were clearly visible for the world to see, but it made me smile inwardly to know that my breasts were considered large for someone of my petite and slight stature. I reveled in the satisfaction of knowing that they were far larger in proportion to my body than hers were in comparison to her figure.

While dramatically flipping my hair behind my shoulders and out of the way, I managed to inconspicuously squeeze just a bit more water out of the long strands. My eyes kept watch of Noah's reaction as the cold liquid hit my already hardened nipples that were now no longer hidden beneath my thick hair.

Furious, Danica's eyes flashed fire.

"Seriously?" she bellowed. "Are you seriously going to strut around like you're in a wet tee shirt contest?"

I gave her an innocent look.

A very frustrated Danica gave Noah a pleading expression of dismay.

"Noah, honey," she cooed. "Will you please ask your guest to take off that wet shirt?"

I snuck a glance at his manhood. It was easy to see that his body was reacting to the sight of my nipples and I was enjoying it immensely. Not just because it irritated Danica, but because it was satisfying to know that he did have an attraction to me after all. Sauntering as close to him as I dared without getting so close that the she-wolf could become a genuine physical threat, I looked up at him and gave him a wan smile.

"Does it really matter?" I asked as I continued to inch closer to the side of Noah where she wasn't. "After all, I'm a nobody who his majesty feels obligated to protect. Surely, my presence isn't even noticed by my lord and his ladyship."

"Cute," he said as he looked down at me with smoldering, lust filled eyes.

I felt mildly empowered to know that I had the ability to torture him in such a way. He deserved to be tortured after rejecting me because of my breeding. He deserved to be tormented for selecting that evil she-wolf as his bedmate. Even if he didn't intend for her to be his permanent mate, Oscar made it clear that they were sleeping together.

"Noah!" Danica screeched.

My nature was far from that of an exhibitionist. This type of behavior was foreign to me. Then, most of the emotions I'd felt since meeting him were unfamiliar ones.

I justified my actions by reminding myself that it wasn't as if what he was seeing was new to his eyes. After all, it was Noah who found me sitting in total nakedness on the lakeshore by that headless body and carried me back to the cabin. Now, with the situation being less dire, he was allowing his body to react in a way that it would have never done with my recently assaulted nakedness. It made me feel darned good.

I knew that I was pushing my luck by

behaving in such a way in front of Danica. I'd already witnessed how volatile she could be when provoked. I had no doubt that her werewolf self was still prevalent in her system since it was only a matter of hours since she'd shifted. If it came down to a battle, I was certain that I wouldn't fare as good as Kenzie did. Between the fact that my human strength couldn't hold a candle to her werewolf strength and that I wasn't as strong as Kenzie or schooled in animal wrestling, I knew I wouldn't stand a chance.

So, why did I continue to taunt her?

I had no explanation for it. I simply put it in the same confusion box as all of the other out of character things that I'd done since meeting Noah.

He looked down at me and said in a low, pleading tone, "Can you please get rid of that shirt?"

Hearing him do her bidding sent me over the edge of reason. My blood boiled with jealous resentment as I looked into his eyes. They were soft and pleading. It was clear that he had no desire to argue any longer with the she-wolf. Nor did he wish to have trouble with me.

As irrational as it was, instead of feeling sorry for him, I inwardly cursed him for not taking my side and telling her to take a hike and leave me be. I was so filled with frustration that I barely knew my own mind.

"Is that what you really want?" I asked as I locked eyes with him. When he nodded, I heaved a sigh, pulled the tee shirt over my head, and tossed it at his face while saying, "Okay. Here you go."

I don't know who gasped louder from the shock of my actions, Danica, or Noah. Feeling more than a little satisfied at their reaction, I placed my hands on my hips and cocked my head to the side.

"Now what?" I asked as I feigned a sigh of frustration. "You don't want me to remove anything else, do you?"

When I dramatically gripped the waistband of my shorts to indicate that they were the next thing that I intended to remove, Danica sprang into action. The folly of my childish behavior was immediately apparent when I saw her hands turn claw-like as she flung her outraged bulk toward me.

I may not have been as strong as she was, but I was far more agile and quick on my feet. It was enough to keep a distance between us until Noah could come to his senses and grab Danica around the waist.

I watched as she flailed and kicked to be free. His strength in holding her steady was impressive. When she finally calmed down, he yanked her by the arm out of the room and onto the front porch.

"Get that slut out of here!" the irate

she-wolf screeched. "I mean it, Noah. Either she goes or I go!"

Once again, he spoke in a tone that was difficult for me to hear. I could only tell that he wasn't saying what she wanted him to say when she screamed her indignation before storming off to her car and peeling down the drive.

It wasn't until he reentered the house and stood staring at my bare breasts that I came to my senses and realized that I still didn't have a top on. Feeling foolish, I covered my nipples with my arms as I rushed to retrieve my tee shirt.

"Don't bother on my account," he said as he moved in front of me.

I could feel the heat of his body on my flesh as he pulled me close so that my breasts were crushed against his hard chest. The heat of his breath caressed my face as he lowered his lips to meet mine.

I had no idea that kisses could be so delectable.

With our lips still locked, he swept me into his strong arms and strode into his bedroom. I gave no resistance as he lowered me onto the bed with such ease that anyone watching would have thought that I weighed nothing.

His eyes surveyed my naked breasts with appreciation as he verbally praised their beauty. He latched his lips onto a hard,

protruding nipple and seductively suckled
while he gently pulled my shorts and panties
from my hips and down my legs. I held his
head to my breast and raised my hips to aid
him in his task while I closed my eyes and
reveled in the sensation.

I'd had sex with men in the past. In
fact, I'd lived for several years with a man
who I was engaged to. Never had coupling
felt like this. My breasts were screaming
with pleasure and my womanhood was
pulsing with desire. I didn't know what to
do. I wanted him to keep doing what he was
doing to my needy breasts, but my
womanhood was about to drive me mad for
want of him.

I finally vocalized my desires.

With a low, deep throated chuckle, he
slid his hand down to my sensitive nub and
let his fingers pleasure me while his mouth
and other hand continued to enjoy and
tantalize my breasts. It satiated my need for
a while, but soon the orgasms that his
ministrations caused weren't quite enough.
Nothing but
having him inside of me would satisfy the
insatiable need that he'd caused.

Switching his hands to my breasts, he
kneaded them with a seductive passion that
made me not miss his suckling while he
lowered his mouth to my womanhood. I
gasped with shocked delight as his tongue

did things that caused me to feel like I was about to explode. Oral sex of that nature was something I'd never experienced with a man before and I liked it. I liked it a lot.

Feeling almost punished by his delay of entering me, I verbally demanded that he do so.

To my surprise, he'd managed to remove his pants and shirt sometime during our foreplay. I'd been so wrapped up in reveling in my own sexual pleasure, that I never even noticed him disrobing.

"You're completely healed, correct?" he said in a deep, sultry tone.

"Yes," I gasped.

My body shuddered with anticipation as I watched his strong shoulders support his torso as he carefully drove his manhood into me. It was done slowly and sweetly at first. Then, as we settled into a unified rhythm, it became more heightened and aggressive.

I'd never peaked in unison with my sex partner until then. It was a sensation that I won't forget or can ever be matched.

29

We lay, peacefully, in each other's arms after making love into the night. As I listened to the steady beating of his heart while he slept, I wondered if the fact that he'd been such a powerfully virile lover was due to his recent shift from being a werewolf or if it was something that I'd have to look forward to on a regular basis. I hoped it was the latter.

I have no idea how long I reveled in sheer ecstasy over finally getting him to want me before I fell into a deep, dream filled slumber.

I rarely remembered my dreams, but this time it was so vivid that it seemed real.

I stood in the middle of a sea of wildflowers with scents that were both intoxicating and alluring. Closing my eyes, I inhaled through my nose until my lungs could hold no more. Feeling delightfully heady from nature's sweet floral bouquet, I slowly and reluctantly exhaled.

When I opened my eyes, a tall, rugged

middle-aged highlander male stood before me. He wore the traditional kilt that fell just below his knees and thick homespun wool socks that protected his calves. A tam hat fell over the right side of a head that sported thick, jet black hair with wisps of grey running through it. A tartan sash over his broad chest finished the look of authenticity. Although I'd never seen his likeness before, I inherently knew that he was Logan McKean, my great, great, great, great grandfather.

"Aye, lass, you came," he said with a gentle smile.

Looking for validation that I was correct in who I felt he was, I questioningly said, "Grandfather Logan?"

"In the flesh," he said with a chuckle before adding, "of sorts."

I looked around and asked, "Where are we?"

"You are standing in your ancestor's homeland, lass," he said, "Back in the day when magic reigned supreme."

"There really was such a time?" I questioningly said.

"Aye, there was," he said with a nod.

Although the place was beautiful and it felt right and natural to be there with him, I had to ask, "Why am I here?"

"The Cailleach who bound our pack wishes to speak with you," he explained.

"Cailleach?" I repeated.

"I ken you would call her a witch or crone," he replied as he started walking toward the base of a nearby low mountain. "We risk her ire by keeping her waiting. Step lively, lass."

"Isn't this a dream?" I asked as I hurried to catch up.

"Dreams take place in alternate realities, ban-ogha," he replied.

"Ban-ogha?" I repeated.

"It means granddaughter," he explained with a touch of obvious patience. "I am called seanair, which means grandfather. In the case of being removed by several generations, you would say sean-seanair."

I scowled as I tried to absorb the odd sounding words and then nodded as
I asked, "Is it okay if I just call you Grandfather Logan?"

He gave as soft smile and nod of his head as he lightly placed his hand on the small of my back to nudge me into motion in the direction he wanted to go.

When we'd reached the mouth of a barely visible cave, I stopped and looked at our surroundings. They'd shifted from rolling meadow to dense woods.

"This reminds me of the place where Kenzie and I hid from our would be abductors," I announced as I followed him through the cave's mouth.

I let him lead me deep into the bowels

193

of the cave without a second thought. As we moved along, torches would ignite to provide us with the ability to see where we were going. I accepted this like I'd accepted everything else that was happening. No matter what Logan said, I chose to believe I was dreaming and, in a dream, anything goes.

After passing through several caverns that took us deep into the bowels of the hillside, we came upon one that was clearly occupied by someone who dealt with the occult. As I looked around, I marveled at how closely its decor resembled the caves of witches in the stories and movies that I'd grown up with. They say that there was a bit of truth behind every fairy tale. From what I could see, that was a correct assumption.

Although torches lined the walls of the cave and an aggressive fire rose from the pit in its center, it still took a few moments for my eyes to spot the old woman sitting in an alcove at the far side of the cozy cave.

"This be she?" she said in a scratchy voice that hinted of years and years of use and held an accent that didn't match Logan's. "Bring the gal hither."

I gave him a questioning look before allowing him to escort me by my upper arm until I stood so close to the ancient looking crone that I could smell the spiciness of her breath.

With her back hunched low and hands that were disfigured from arthritis or some other crippling affliction, almost black eyes that were small and recessed into boney sockets, and unkempt grey hair, she made a frightening sight. Yet, I wasn't afraid.

I imagined her scratchy voice eking out the saying from a children's movie, "Double, double, toil and trouble" while stirring a cauldron of boiling brew and giggled.

"Do ye find me humorous, gal?" the old crone asked.

Shocked and annoyed with myself for allowing my thoughts to get carried away to the extent that I mindlessly vocalized them, I looked at her with wide eyes and shook my head.

"No, I don't," I quickly assured her. "I'm sorry. The décor made me remember a movie that I saw when I was a child and it brought me joy," I semi-lied. -After all. I'd told the truth in stating that I'd been reminded of the movie, but I left out that it was imagining her stirring the cauldron that had made me giggle.

She looked me up and down with a scrutinizing glower that I found unsettling.

When she was finally satisfied, she said, "Ye have inherited the strong gene. I can see why they seek ye for mating."

I gave both her and my grandfather a puzzled look.

"I don't understand," I said. "Doesn't the gene simply pass down from generation to generation?"

She nodded. "Aye, it does, but it is noght the same strength. In some, like yerself, 'tis strong. In others 'tis weak. It skips generations." She was silent for a moment before adding, "Ye have the sight as well. That has noght been passed on for nary a century."

I found myself wondering how this old crone knew so much about my family lineage when she surprised me by letting me know.

"Did he noght tell you that I be yer grandmother ten times removed?" she asked.

"Ten times?" I gasped as I studied her more closely. No one can live that long. Then, it was a dream...

As logan had done during our first meeting, she read my thoughts and said, "This is no dream, gal. Noght in the way that ye think of dreams. Yer in an alternate reality where time behaves different. In yer reality, I be nawhit but bones, as be he."

"I appear as a ghost," he said with humor.

When she gave him an impatient glower, he wiped the smile from his face and cleared his throat.

"Do noght take our meeting lightly, gal," she sternly said. "It taking place here instead of there, makes it noght less real."

196

I could hear her words, but had difficulty focusing on them. A sudden tingling in my body made me restless and eager to return to my own reality.

Fidgeting to ease the sensation that I could almost label erotic, I said, "I'm unsure of the purpose of our meeting."

"I see ye are being pulled back," she observed with a frown. "I shall be brief. Ye must stand firm and not succumb to the temptations of allowing them to take charge of yer destiny. Ye were born to be a queen, not a serf. Stand firm, lass and protect yourself. Do noght settle for less than what ye deserve. Keep our line strong and pure."

I was unclear of what she was referring to, but, at that moment, I didn't care. The pull of the erotic sensation was almost overwhelming. I had no choice but to give in. The world swirled around me as the cave and its occupants disappeared and I was bathed in darkness.

As sleep receded and I grew more alert, the pleasure of Noah's mouth on my womanhood made me squirm with satisfaction.

Reaching down to place my fingers through his hair, I openly moaned with desire. Realizing that I was awake, he grew more aggressive with his ministrations, incorporating moving his strong fingers in and out of me while his tongue worked hard to bring me to erotic heights.

When I bucked my hips out of frustration and need of more, he quickly shifted his body so that he could enter me with a lusty fervor. His thrusts were strong and deep enough to make me gasp as he teased my g-spot with regularity.

I climaxed several times before he did, which seemed to bring him manly satisfaction. I secretly chuckled at the importance a man took in being proven a good lover. He actually was a good lover and didn't need reassurance, but I gave it to him anyway with my words and my body's reactions.

When he was done, he lept from the bed and wandered into the ensuite bathroom while tossing the words, "Good morning" over his shoulder. I greeted him back while I lay in satiated bliss and admired the contour of his muscular back and perfectly shaped buttocks as he disappeared through the bathroom entrance.

When I heard the shower turn on, I mouth formed a mischievous grin as I lept from the bed. Without waiting for an invitation, I joined him in the shower. He was surprised at first, but, then, he accepted my presence and shared the body wash with me.

I closed my eyes and enjoyed his hands massaging suds all over my back and buttocks. I was surprised when I spread my legs wide for him to cleanse my womanhood that it throbbed with a hint of desire once more. After such an aggressive sexual start to the day, I would have thought there'd be no need for more so soon.

When his hands reached my breasts, my nipples came alive. It must have been what triggered his libido because that's when he stopped washing me and began to devour me as if he'd been without a woman for at least a decade. His mouth moved about my body, tasting, nibbling, and teasing until I thought I'd explode with need. When he finally lifted me up and braced me against the shower wall so that he could enter me, I wrapped my legs around
his waist and clamped my arms tight around his strong neck.

I'd never made love in the shower before. The feel of the water beating on our bodies as he pumped his large, hard manhood into me made it even sexier than when we were in bed. I decided to make this a habit.

I could feel him growing larger inside of me. To my surprise, he didn't release. Instead, he pulled out and turned me so that my back was to him. I gasped as I felt him enter me again. It was marvelously different, yet equally erotic.

It must have been the same for him

because within a matter of a few thrusts he was releasing.

We finished our shower in silence, but I didn't mind. My head was swimming with visions of our future together.

I hadn't a very fulfilling sex life with my fiancé. It improved as time wore on and we got to know each other's likes and dislikes, but it never reached the heights that Noah and I were at from the start.

If Noah and I started out like this, I could only imagine where we'd be in another year or so.

30

Oscar and Kenzie had arrived by the time I was dressed and out of the bedroom. Eager to share my joy with my friend, I entered the living room with a broad smile on my face. It quickly dissipated when my eyes landed on Danica snuggling close to Noah as if they were the couple of the century. Not knowing what to do, I stopped in my tracks and gave him a *what the hell?* glower. To my shock and disappointment, he worriedly pursed his lips and looked away.

I wanted to fade into nothingness. I worried that the fact that I'd been used as a sex object throughout the night and into the morning had become common knowledge. Although I didn't want anyone to know, I especially worried about Danica finding out. What a feather in her mean girl cap that would be.

I felt used and cheap.

Kenzie moved close to me and asked in a soft tone, "What's the matter?"

I forced a smile as I replied, "Nothing. I just didn't think Danica was here too. That's all."

My friend slowly nodded as she whispered, "I get it. She's a real pain in the ass, but she's a permanent fixture. Or, at least Oscar seems to think so. He laments over it daily."

"He shouldn't," I snipped as I moved toward the kitchen. "If you ask me, they're perfect for each other." Putting a light skip into my step, I glanced over my shoulder at Noah as I said as light-heartedly as I could manage, "I'm
starving. Let's raid the kitchen."

"Oh! Oh!" she excitedly said. "There's this really cute breakfast place near Oscar's house. It's called... are you ready? Harry's Breakfast Place and, yes, it's owned by none other than Harry himself. Isn't that a hoot? It's not very imaginative and even less to look at, but the food is fantastic. Anyway, we went there and I grabbed you some blueberry pancakes and bacon."

"Yum," I said with genuine appreciation.

A smug smile formed on her face as she said, "I thought you'd like it."

"I think I'd like to eat outside," I mused as I glowered in Noah's direction. "If I'm allowed out, that is."

"I don't see why not," Oscar said with a

friendly grin as he presented me with the takeout box containing my breakfast.

"I'll grab some fresh coffee and meet you out back," Kenzie offered. "Noah has a pretty nice set up for entertaining behind the house."

"I'm sure he does," I grumbled as I accepted the takeout box from Oscar with a wan smile and walked with steadfast determination past Noah and his she-wolf toward the back door. I kept my head held high and didn't spare them even the slightest glance.

"Grab me a cup of coffee too, honey, and I'll join you," Oscar said as Kenzie headed for the coffee pot.

"You'll do no such thing," she said with faux aggravation. "I need a little alone time with my girl."

I hid a grin while I imagined the scowl on Oscar's face over being forced to remain in Danica's company as I stepped through the door onto the back patio. The early morning air hinted of the heat that was to come. I appreciated the four seasons that Pennsylvania offered, but I enjoyed the summers most.

Sitting with my back to the house and my face lifted toward the newly risen sun, I closed my eyes and listened to Kenzie make her way out of the house with a French Press and two mugs for the rich, aromatic brew that it contained.

Easing herself into the chair opposite me at the quaint bistro table that Noah had positioned in the corner of his entertainment patio, she placed her elbows on the tabletop and rested her chin in her hands as she said with a firm tone, "Okay. Talk."

"What?" I asked as I opened my takeout box and dove into the pancakes like some starving waif.

"What's wrong?" she asked. "Don't say it's because Danica's here."

I shrugged my shoulders as I fought back the urge to sob while trying not to choke on my pancakes.

Seeing the state that I was in, she sat back and scowled.

"What happened?" she asked with genuine concern.

"He's an ass," I murmured as I stuffed more food into my mouth.

"Besides that," she continued. When I said nothing, she said, "Come on. Get it off your chest before you choke to death on those lovely pancakes."

"I was a fool," I whimpered as I swallowed the food I'd shoveled into my mouth and put the fork down. "I'm confused, disappointed, and pissed off. Over my time with him, I've grown to love him. It wasn't intentional. It just sort of snuck up on me. I suffered in silence because he didn't seem to want to do anything but protect me from the werewolves. Last night he finally showed differently. We spent the night making love and today... well... You see today."

"Shit," she hissed. "Damn the man."

"It's my fault," I admitted as I picked the fork back up and stabbed at what was left of my breakfast. "I teased him and he took the bait."

Her brows raised, but she didn't press me to tell her how I'd teased. When I didn't volunteer the information, she said, "Believe it or not, he occupied a good deal of the conversation between Oscar and me last night. He thinks Noah is battling his attraction to you big time. He said he's never seen his brother behave with a woman like he has with you."

"Behave how?" I asked. "Before last night, all he did was ignore me."

"He's never taken on the task of protecting a female from being taken by the werewolves before," she said. "He uses the excuse that he's obligated because you were staying at his cabin, but that's bull. You aren't the first female to stay at his cabin and be taken by the werewolves. According to Oscar, there were a few before you. Not recently, mind you, but spread out over the years. He did nothing to stop it. In fact, he claimed that it was not his place to interfere with the actions of another pack. He also said that although he'd never do it, in some ways, he understood the need to do what was necessary to keep the werewolves from extinction."

I looked at her as if she had three heads as I frowned in thought and said, "I don't get it."

"He's into you, Lisa," she said with an exasperated huff. "Get with the program."

"Yeah, sure," I scoffed. "He's so into me that he screwed me for half the night and then again this morning only to run into Danica's arms as soon as he left the bedroom."

"Half the night?" she said with a hint of awe. "It's a wonder you were up to it after…"

"I'm fine," I interrupted her. "In fact, I'm better than fine and, if you don't mind, I'd rather not talk about the attack or last night again. I just want to go home and forget about it all."

"Go home?" she worriedly said.

"My great, great, great, great grandfather Logan came to me in the night," I offered. "He took me to some cave to meet the witch who bound my people. She was going to tell me something, but Noah interrupted things. I think that if I go home and am alone, I'll be able to connect with her and find out what she wants me to know."

"She didn't get to tell you anything?" Kenzie said with a hint of disappointment.

I sipped at my steaming coffee before saying, "Only a few things like the gene that I have skips generations and my psychic ability even more generations. She called it *the gift*."

"I agree," Kenzie firmly said. "It is a gift."

After another good gulp, I added, "Oh, and that I was born to be a queen and not to let them subdue me or something like that. I need clarity before I can understand it all. I need to connect with her again."

"I think that's a good idea," she said, "but I don't want you going home. What if you came and stayed with Oscar and me? We can give you the space you need to make your connections."

It was something that I'd already considered, but I wasn't comfortable suggesting. Now that she'd made the offer, I had to know how Oscar would feel about it.

"Would he be good with that?" I asked.

"It was Oscar who suggested it," she replied with a smug smile.

31

The sound of Noah and Oscar arguing in the living room could be heard out onto the patio. Although Kenzie didn't seem as surprised as I was with their reason for their mini war, we both had to snap our mouths shut to keep from giggling as we listened to them battle over the fact that Oscar wanted to remove me from Noah's care.

"You'll leave her here and that's that," Noah bellowed.

"She wants to go with Kenzie," Oscar bellowed back. "She's not a child, Noah. If she wants to leave, let her leave."

"She's not safe," Noah growled.

"With me?" Oscar said with an outraged tone. "Are you saying that you're the only one capable of keeping her safe?"

"She stays here," Noah demanded.

I lept from my chair and stormed back into the house. Planting myself just inches away from him, I looked Noah in the eye and hissed, "I'll go where I want to go. I'm not your property."

"But..." he began.

Looking around, I saw no sign of Danica.

"Where's your she-wolf?" I asked.

"She's not my she-wolf and she's gone," he replied.

I looked him up and down with as much disdain as I could muster.

"You're something else," I sneered.

Oscar opened his mouth to speak, but Kenzie pulled on his arm to stop him.

"Let her at him," she softly urged. "The man had sex with her last night and this morning only to ignore her while cuddling Danica."

I sucked in air as I listened to my friend divulge information that I thought I'd shared with her in private. I wanted to reprimand her, but it didn't seem the time or to be appropriate for the occasion. Besides, her divulging that bit of information to Oscar triggered an avalanche of disdain from him toward Noah and the arguing renewed full force.

"You did what?" Oscar blurted with disgust. "I thought I knew you, brother, but I guess not. Never in a million years did I think you'd stoop so low as to use a woman like that."

"I didn't use her," Noah protested.

"No?" I asked as I placed my hands on my hips. "What would you call it, then?"

He looked from his brother, to Kenzie and then to me. It was clear that he was uncomfortable with the topic, but he saw no way of avoiding it.

Heaving a sigh of resignation, he hesitantly said in a soft tone, "We made love."

"Are you in the habit of *making love* to a woman one minute and then ignoring her while you fondle another woman the next?" Kenzie angrily asked. She made sure to get her point across by emphasizing the words making love.

"I wasn't fondling Danica," he forcefully said. "She was fondling me."

"Oh, that makes it better?" I incredulously roared.

He shook his head.

"It doesn't," he said, "but I don't know what to do."

He gave a reluctant look in Oscar and Kenzie's direction. I got the impression that he longed for them to disappear so that he could speak to me privately. I inwardly smiled when I realized that they had no intention of affording him that opportunity.

"You need to make a decision, brother," Oscar demanded. "I won't stand by and watch you use this poor girl like that. She deserves better."

"Yes, she does," Noah admitted. "If she hadn't gone to the cabin, she'd have better. She'd have a normal life instead of being a target for every male werewolf seeking a mate."

"Maybe not," I offered as I remembered the words of the old crone.

"What?" Noah asked with surprise.

"I believe in fate and karma," I replied. "You can't be sure that it wasn't supposed to happen. Maybe, if I didn't go to your cabin, my werewolf gene would be discovered some other way."

"That's right," Kenzie agreed. "Instead of lamenting over it, you should be grateful that it surfaced when you were able to know her. Otherwise, she'd be the mate of some unknown werewolf and you'd be left in the cold. Then, you don't seem to want to make a move, so I guess it doesn't matter, anyway."

I watched as the color rose in his cheeks. Her words were like a slap in Noah's frustrated face.

I wanted to hurt him as much as he hurt me. From what I could see, Kenzie was correct in her claim that he had feelings for me. They just weren't strong enough for him to go against the wishes of his pack and give up Danica. I should have understood, but I was too hurt. All I could feel was the overwhelming need to strike out at him.

"Speaking of being paired," I purposefully cooed, "didn't you say you had a fella in mind for me?"

Surprised enough to be taken aback by my unexpected question, it took Oscar a moment to regain his senses enough to say, "Yes, I do. I was thinking of Caleb Smythe. He's a newly appointed pack leader near the southern border. I understand he's shopping for a mate."

"I've seen his picture," Kenzie blurted out. "He's cute, Lisa. You could do a lot worse."

"Is he kind and considerate?" I asked as I glowered at Noah. "That's more important to me. I've had my fill of selfish asses."

I felt a smug satisfaction as I watched my one-night-stand lover struggle to hold his tongue as he listened to me converse about a potential mate with his brother and my friend.

"He runs an animal shelter," Oscar said. "He takes in dogs, cats, and sometimes horses."

Kenzie's brows raised as she said with obvious approval, "You have to be kind at heart to run something like that."

"When can I meet him?" I asked.

"This afternoon, if you'd like," Oscar said as he dropped into a nearby chair. "I happen to volunteer once a month at shelters in the state. His is the next on the rotation."

"You're sure he's not already involved with a woman?" I grilled. "The last thing I want is to become a closet lover."

That dig was directed at Noah and I knew that he knew it. From the looks on Kenzie and Oscar's faces, I guessed they realized it too.

Not wanting my slams to lose momentum, I continued with, "Can we leave now so that I can get cleaned up? I'd like to look my best when you introduce me."

Oscar stood up and, with his eyes on Noah, nervously said, "Sure thing."

Kenzie clearly didn't feel the guilt that her lover felt as she waltzed past Noah without so much as a glance his way while urging me to follow her to their SUV.

32

I was more nervous than I could imagine ever being as I sat in the waiting room in the veterinary office of Caleb Smyth's rescue shelter while awaiting his arrival. With a good number of animals in need of care, Kenzie and Oscar immediately went to work. Left alone, my thoughts went to the absurdity of the situation. I was literally there to meet a man who was openly shopping for a wife. Or, as the werewolves put it, a mate.

Was I really going to go through with this?

I'd thought that when I broke my engagement with Rob that I'd wait a while before I let love come my way. As for marriage, it wasn't something that I was really anxious to enter into. After all, as long as I continued to live the way I'd chosen for the last few years, I could see no issue with finances in my future. I'd inherited a tidy sum from my grandmother and the novels that I wrote padded the money pot.

Unfortunately, I saw no other option. If I didn't select a mate on my own, I was at risk of being captured and mated to someone who I abhorred. Anyway I looked at it, there was no escaping my fate. My werewolf genes saw to that.

I regretted not getting the full story from the old crone. My intuition was screaming at me that there was more to who I was and what I was about than I was grasping. She'd said that I was meant to be a queen. That made no sense to me, yet I felt that there was truth to her statement.

I was deep in thought when the sound of a man clearing his throat
brought me back to reality. My breath caught in my chest as my eyes climbed the tall, well-built figure of a man until they reached the smiling face of the very handsome Caleb Smythe. I found myself immediately comparing his good looking, all-American-boy-next-door- let-me-model-your-Armani-suit-for-GQ look to that of Noah's rugged, sexy bad-boy-I'll-sport-your-Calvin-Klein-jeans-for-the-camera-while-bare-chested-and-wearing-an-open-leather-jacket look.

It was just my luck that I preferred the bad boy look.

"You must be Lisa," he said in a smooth, voice that sounded far too confident and well trained for my taste.

I nodded and returned his smile.

"I take it you are Caleb," I said as I extended my hand for him to shake.

"The one and only," he said as he accepted my offer. Instead of shaking it, he bent low and let his lips lightly brush against my flesh.

I inwardly giggled at the corny, antiquated gesture, but simply smiled my appreciation outwardly. After all, he was trying to make a good impression to someone who he had absolutely no knowledge of. Hadn't I insisted on going home and making myself beautiful for that very same reason? I also had to admit to myself that I was being a bit bias because of the feelings that I'd foolishly developed for Noah. I needed to push them back and give this man a fair chance.

It was drizzling rain with a slight chill in the air accompanying it, hinting that fall was approaching. I don't know why, but I'd worn the red cape that Kenzie had tossed over me during the werewolf attack. At the time, it seemed like the perfect choice of outerwear. It was made of wool which was a good repellant to the raindrops and it was the right weight to ward off the chill. The fact that it annoyed Noah that I took it was an added bonus. Oscar gave me a puzzled look as I pulled it over my shoulders before exchanging an odd look with Noah, but he made no comment about my choice of outer attire.

As I sat across from Caleb chatting about the benevolent work he did for animals while analyzing the unsettling look in his eyes, I questioned my decision to wear it. I felt a touch like Little Red Riding Hood as the wolf attempted to lure her into his trap. It wasn't until Kenzie joined us that I realized that I'd subconsciously pulled the cape closed in front.

There was something unsettling about this man. It may have been the fact that his smile didn't reach his eyes. I felt a hidden agenda behind all that delicious handsomeness.

When I mentioned it to Kenzie later that day, she insisted that it was simply me resisting the notion of pairing with anyone other than Noah, but I knew better.

I rarely got that gut warning about a person, place, or thing. This was the second one in a month. The first one was when I met Oscar and Noah. I didn't take notice of it and look what happened. I wasn't about to make that mistake again.

I gave him my polite attention while I kept an ear on the alert for the return of my friends. The uneasiness in my gut was spreading throughout my body. By the time I spotted Kenzie entering the room out of the corner of my eye, I could hardly contain it.

Jumping to my feet, I interrupted his attempt to invite me to dinner by saying in a rather loud voice, "Here's Kenzie. Have you met? She's a veterinary as well. She's been helping Oscar."

Surprised by my unceremonious interruption to his dinner invitation, he stammered, "Why... no, I haven't met her."

I watched him rapidly take control of his emotions so that by the time he faced Kenzie, he gave the impression of being relaxed and pleased for the introduction.

Kenzie fell into an easy conversation with Caleb, which gave me the opportunity to study him more closely. If not for that gut instinct warning me that something was amiss, I would have thought him to be a handsome and polite man who was worth considering taking as my mate. Unfortunately, no matter how many ways or times that I tried to explain it away as foolish nervousness on my part, that nagging warning simply wouldn't dissipate. Instead, it grew stronger by the minute.

By the time Oscar joined us, I was more than ready to leave. Sadly, my friends had a different idea. Where he'd failed in cajoling me into a dinner date, Caleb had managed to slip the invitation into his conversation with Oscar and Kenzie. Needless to say, they accepted.

We spent the few hours left before

dinner touring his facilities. I had to admit that I found the size and condition of the place impressive. Caleb professed to be a stickler for organization and cleanliness and it showed in every inch of his facility. I'd only visited a few rescue places in my day, so I had little to compare it to. The few I had visited were much smaller in size and distinctly inferior in both cleanliness and organization.

When we'd finished touring the main part of the facility, he took us to an area that was marked "restricted". Behind those doors I was amazed to discover a few rooms that contained several cages with convalescing wildlife. In one room there was an eagle and a few rabbits. Another hosted two foxes who'd had the misfortune of getting caught in a trap, but the good fortune of being discovered and rescued before the trapper returned to check on things. The final room we entered contained an enormous wolf with a broken leg.

As I approached the cage, it snarled its warning. To my surprise, instead of stopping, I steadily continued until only the wire of the cage separated my face from his. Clearly, my time with Snow had altered my perception of what was and wasn't dangerous.

I locked eyes with the beast until his snarling ceased. Afterward, he openly sniffed at my face and hair as best as he could from within his confines.

"How did he break his leg?" I asked as I turned to face my three shocked companions.

"He doesn't allow anyone near that cage," Caleb said with awe. Grabbing a long handled gripper, he added, "We use this to feed him and sedate him when it's time to check on his progress."

"Really?" I said with surprise as I turned back to inspect the wolf more closely. "He seems calm enough."

"With you, maybe," Oscar said with a chuckle, "but he almost took my hand off when I set that leg."

"Well," I said with a tone that indicated how foolish his statement was, "he was in pain."

Oscar vigorously shook his head.

"It was more than just being in pain," he said. "Most of the time, wolves bond with us. It's on rare occasions that we meet what we'd call a rebel. You have before you, one of the rebels. We don't meet wolves of his nature often, thank goodness."

I slid my fingers through the wired opening so that the wolf could lick them.

"That's so difficult to believe," I mused.

"Lisa," Kenzie warned, "don't press your luck."

I reluctantly pulled my fingers away

from my canine admirer, but not before I scratched him on the top of his head between his ears, like I'd done with Snow on multiple occasions.

"Damn!" Caleb said with shocked awe. "You have a definite way with animals."

"Not really," I confessed while Kenzie choked back a laugh. "In fact, I have little experience with them. I've only recently been exposed to wolves, though." Remembering Snow and his dedication to my well-being, I added,
"They seem to like me."

"I see that," he mused as he studied me with more interest than he'd shown all day.

33

Don't ask me why, but for some reason I thought that Caleb was going to cook our dinner for us. Perhaps it was because of his smooth confidence with all aspects of his animal care facility that I assumed that he'd be proficient in all areas of life.

Not true.

The man confessed that he was hard pressed to make eggs and toast and, then, the eggs had to be scrambled.

His saving grace was the fact that he had a full-time cook. I don't know when he managed to inform this cook that there would be company for dinner, but when we entered the main house just as dusk was approaching, the prepared table was set with delicate fine china that looked like it was a family heirloom that had been tenderly cared for since the early nineteenth century. Crystal wine glasses and water goblets reflected the soft and gentle glow of candlelight that was strategically placed on either side of the low flowered center piece.

As I admired the table setting, I noticed that there were two more places prepared than there were diners. When I pointed this out to him, he informed me that he was expecting his cousin and his longtime friend to join us.

Realizing that I'd be attending a small dinner party instead of just an evening meal after an afternoon of touring his facility, I was thankful that I'd taken the precaution of stopping home and putting on something presentable. The black wide leg pants and silver cashmere cardigan that I wore were versatile enough to pass for a fine afternoon or casual dinner party wear. I'd even slipped on a gold and onyx cuff bracelet with matching earrings that, although fairly simple, could easily be used to dress and outfit up. My only regret was that I'd worn sensible shoes instead of delicate heels that would have really made a statement. Since he'd asked us to remove our shoes to protect the floors of his turn of the century home from the fact that we'd walked through a goodly amount of dirt that suffered from being rained upon, I decided that it didn't matter about the heels.

Having assisted him for several years with the compound's veterinary needs, Oscar was invited into the main house on multiple occasions. Because he was familiar with its layout, our host suggested that he give

Kenzie a quick tour while he and I got to know each other a little better as we waited for the last of the dinner guests to arrive.

I accepted the glass of Chardonnay that was offered to me as I allowed Caleb to lead me into what I assumed was once the parlor of the home, but was now a casual living room. It's wooden floor was partially covered by a thick wool carpet that accentuated the floor's gleaming finish. Rich, mahogany woodwork framed walls that sported several large windows to let in the light and wide, majestic doorways. The thing that immediately caught my eye was a tasteful stained glass panel on the top of the main window that depicted a hunting scene with wolves instead of hounds.

"This is my favorite room in the house," he explained. "It isn't the biggest or the best, but I enjoy the way the sun reflects the colors of the stained glass window on bright days."

"Your home is lovely," I said.

It was not only in pristine condition, but it was what I would refer to as being immaculate. I thought about my turn of the century house and found myself ashamed of the dust and clutter that I'd allowed to accumulate in the less used parts of the house. I didn't need a tour to know that wasn't the case with this place. I had no doubt that every inch was dust and clutter free.

"How do you keep up with the maintenance of this house?" I asked as I positioned myself on the end cushion of an extremely inviting sofa. "You have a pretty busy schedule and I imagine the care of something this large and this old is time consuming."

He nodded as he said, "I have a groundskeeper and a small house keeping staff. This land has been in my family since before the revolutionary war. Before this house was built in eighteen-twenty, there was a smaller, salt box type home that my ancestors dwelled in. I used the bones of it to create the office for the sanctuary."

Duly impressed, I said, "Really? How much land do you have?"

"We're down to one-hundred and fifty acres," he said with a sigh. "Originally, we owned the entire side of the mountain, but I needed funds to keep the place going and, well, you can probably figure it out from there."

"I would think you'd be getting grants," I mused.

"I do... now," he admitted. "It wasn't the case in the beginning. It took time for me to find my footing and direction. While that was going on, I was forced to sell off land to keep myself afloat." After a moment, he added, "I didn't sell off all of the mountain. Some was done by my ancestors. Family troubles and things like the depression hit us hard. The estate was down to two-hundred and fifty acres by the time I inherited."

"So, you are okay now, right?" I asked as if I was in need of being reassured.

He gave me that warm, handsome smile that never quite reached his eyes as he said, "I assure you that I am more than okay now. You need have no worry in that department."

Realizing that he was referring to his financial stability due to the possibility of us pairing up, I grew flustered. Feeling my face heat up, I turned away in hopes that he wouldn't notice.

Moving to sit next to me, he gently pulled my chin with his long, slender fingers until I was looking into his deep set hazel eyes that were shaped in a way that made me think of a wolf or another type of canine. I jolted with surprise when, for the first time since we'd met that afternoon, I saw real emotion in them.

"This is a new process for you," he said with obvious compassion. "I understand. Our ways are not the same as the rest of society. Necessity causes for strange customs."

"It's been done throughout the ages," I found myself saying. "I just didn't think it was something that I'd be doing."

"Your werewolf genes demand it be so," he said with conviction. "It's my understanding that you had no idea of your genetics until recently. All of this has to be tough for you."

I nodded, but said nothing.

"Historically, we didn't steal women away to mate with," he said with a hint of disgust. "It offends me simply to admit that it's ever been done." After a moment of silence, he asked, "Do you know what happens when a werewolf whose genetics have been blended with a human tries to shift for the first few times?"

"I understand it can be difficult," I replied.

"Excruciating and cruel is more like it," he spat as he looked off into the distance. "I've seen it happen too many times."

"Yet, you're considering me for a mate," I hesitantly said.

He turned and looked at me with surprise.

"I wouldn't if your genetics were truly blended with those of a human," he said. "I know that I'm supposed to be aiding our people in avoiding extinction, but I'm not as desperate as to do that to someone. Even if I was, I'd never force her into it. It would have to be consensual, and that rarely happens. There's also the matter of acceptance within my pack. As their leader, I'm expected to mate with a pure werewolf."

"But...," I began.

He raised his hand to indicate that I speak no more.

"I know that your genes are magically bound and not blended with humans," he offered. "I can see it in your aura. I'm surprised that Oscar couldn't."

"You see it?" I said with surprise.

"I have the gift of sight," he admitted. "Perhaps that's why."

"I do as well," I eagerly offered.

He nodded and grinned with such genuine sincerity that I couldn't help warming up to him.

"I suspected as much, but I wasn't totally certain," he said. "How does your gift work?"

"I did psychic readings for people on occasion," I said with a shrug. "Nothing major."

"Can you see spirits?" he asked.

"I can," I admitted, "but, to be truthful, I don't like to use my abilities."

"Whyever not?" he asked with surprise.

I looked away as I said, "My former fiancé exploited them for his financial gain."

After a short silence that was so intense that I could have probably cut the air with a knife, had I had one, he said, "I see.

Well, that won't happen with me."

Every inch of my body trembled with panic and confusion at his statement. From all appearances, it looked to me like he was moving forward
with his plans to mate with me.

I quickly said, "I'm not agreeing to mate with you. Not yet, anyway."

His brows raised with surprise, but he said nothing as he waited for me to continue to speak.

Since I was uncomfortable with the entire topic, I had no desire to explain.

The silence between us was tortuous.

He finally broke it by asking, "Can I ask you why you never told Oscar that you are pure werewolf? Not that I mind. He probably would have wanted you for himself if he knew."

Shrugging, I said, "I only just found out and it didn't occur to me. It's all so new to me and I really wasn't looking for a husband. I've been enjoying my freedom. I feel a bit trapped. I hope you understand."

"You do realize that every day you let pass without being sworn to one of us, you run the risk of being abducted and forced to mate with your abductor," he said with earnest.

"I do," I said with regret.

Visions of my headless rapist passed before me as if to reiterate his statement. I hoped that my involuntary shudder was kept inward. I didn't want him to think that the idea of being with him repulsed me, because it didn't. He was kind, gentle and quite handsome. It was clear that he was financially self-sufficient as well. There was also the added bonus that he had the gift like I did. I could do far worse than to pair up with him.

"I'll probably go ahead with it," I mused. Then, realizing that he'd yet to say he actually wanted me in that way, I added, "If you want to, that is."

"I believe I do," he said with a satisfied grin.

"Can we just go slow?" I whimpered as he leaned forward to seal our deal with a kiss. "I mean, I just need a little time to get used to it all. Everything has happened so fast. This is a big commitment. I'm thinking I'll do it, but I want to be sure."

His kiss tasted of rosemary and mint. It was so light and gentle that I was surprised at how powerfully my body reacted to it. I cursed myself for asking him to go slow because when his pheromones mixed with mine, I wanted nothing more than to rip his clothes off right then and there and enjoy his luscious body.

For the first time that day, all thoughts of Noah fled my mind.

Squirming to relieve some of the desire

that had immediately entered my womanhood, I hoped that he interpreted it as timidity instead.

When he apologized for being bold and assured me that he'd take it slow, I sighed with relief that my secret went undiscovered.

Just then, an unsavory looking character who turned out to be the cook appeared at the doorway to announce that the other guests had arrived and that dinner was served. Standing, Caleb offered me his hand to help me up. When I accepted it, he didn't let go. Instead, he slipped it through the crook of his arm and lightly patted it.

"I'd like to announce our pairing at dinner," he whispered as he confidently guided me toward the dining room. "Are you alright with that?"

I looked up at him and sighed. Being so close to him after blending pheromones like we had was almost maddening. I knew that if I tried to speak just then, my efforts to subdue my aroused body would constrict my throat and it might be misconstrued as hesitation. So, I leaned my head against his upper arm instead.

34

The expression Danica wore was both amusing and frightening as she watched Caleb lead me into the chair next to his at the dining table. If he noticed the hate for me in her eyes, he gave no indication of it as he made the introductions around the room.

He seemed mildly surprised to discover that Kenzie and I had already met her. Even so. Other than express his surprise, he made no effort to explore how and why we were acquainted. Instead, he initiated light and interesting table talk about the history of the mountain while we enjoyed several courses that could easily have been served in a five star restaurant. I found the stories that he and Oscar told of their ancestors' practices and beliefs to be both entertaining and intriguing.

It was eye opening to discover that there were significant likenesses and differences in the beliefs and operation of the packs.

Since Caleb was pack leader and

Oscar was second in line behind Noah, the burden of the responsibility eventually entered the conversation. As I listened to them converse about the similarities of expectations of their leader from the pack members, I began to understand a little better the position that Noah was in.

The men were deep in conversation, with Kenzie and I hanging on every word, when Danica blurted out, "You talk of wanting to keep the respect of your people, yet you offer marriage to a mutt!"

The room went so silent that the air felt thick. I looked first at Oscar's reddened face as he struggled to control his temper and then to Caleb, who was surprisingly poised in his reaction to his cousin's outburst.

"My dear Danica," he said with a soft purrlike tone, "Whatever are you talking about?"

Waiving her fork in the air for emphasis, she glowered at me while declaring that I was nothing more than a watered down mutt and he should be ashamed of himself for even contemplating mating with me.

He burst into laughter.

"Wherever did you get such an idea?" he asked with sincerity. "She's nothing of the kind."

Danica opened her mouth to speak

and slammed it shut several times while her mind tried to grasp what her cousin had just declared.

"She is," she finally blurted out. "She's been staying with Noah and Oscar because she peed in the woods and her puny genetics left a scent. She's a mutt, Caleb."

Caleb looked at me with amusement.

"You peed in the woods?" he chuckled. "Somehow, I pictured you as a toilet kind of gal."

I couldn't help giggling at his humor which infuriated Danica all the more.

"I won't stand for it, Caleb," Danica spat. "I'll call a meeting of the wolves and tell them all about your ridiculous plan to mate with this... this thing."

Caleb raised a brow before taking a calm sip from his wine glass. After dabbing at the corner of his mouth with his linen napkin, he slammed the flat of his hand on the table with such force that the crystal rattled with a threatening tone.

His eyes hinted of fire and his face distorted to the extent that he lost his boy-next-door handsomeness as he growled, "I will have you show respect to my intended. If you were informed that she is anything but of a pure bloodline, you were informed incorrectly." His face relaxed to the point of returning to close to normal as he looked at me and said, "Lisa is a rare find, indeed.

She is of an old royal bloodline that was bound so many centuries ago that they have forgotten who they are." Turning back to Danica, he continued with, "Mark my words, cousin, she is purer than you and I put together. I intend to mate with her during the next full moon. She will be your queen and superior in every sense of the word. You will show her the respect that she deserves and you'll show it to her now."

White faced, Danica stared at me with disbelief before turning to Oscar and asking, "Why didn't you tell me?"

Looking just as shocked and confused as she did, he shrugged his shoulders and said, "I had no idea."

Caleb smiled and nodded as he said, "That's where having the gift pays off. Right Lisa? I was able to see the binding in her aura almost immediately." Turning to Danica, he added, "Be grateful that it slipped past Noah. I've not known him to come to the aid of a mutt simply for the sake of it. Clearly, he harbors some sort of affection for her. Had he realized who Lisa is, you might just have had a bit of competition. As it is, I'm in and Noah's out."

"Lisa?" Oscar said after clearing his throat a few times. "Why didn't you tell us?"

"I only just found out," I replied. "I didn't know. In fact, I had no idea werewolves were real until I peed in your woods. This is all new to me."

"She needs time to absorb it all," Kenzie interjected. "I'm not sure it's such a good idea to mate with her so soon. Now that you've claimed her, that should keep the others away. Right?"

Caleb looked to me with surprise as he said, "You don't want to mate that soon?"

I slowly shook my head as I said in a voice that sounded like it belonged to someone other than me, "I don't know what I want right now."

35

I was furious. First I was kept in Noah's home like some kind of prisoner for my protection and, then, Caleb insisted on the same thing.

"I just want to go home," I pouted as I walked with Kenzie back to the SUV. "I may not have been abducted, but I feel like it. I came here to meet him and now I can't leave. It's so wrong."

"You can come back with us," Kenzie offered. "I'll speak to Oscar about it."

"I wish that she could," Oscar said as he approached us from behind. "Unfortunately, I don't hold the power to go against Caleb. The only one who can is another pack leader."

"Like Noah," Kenzie mused.

"Oh, hell no!" I exclaimed without hesitation.

"Listen to me," Oscar said with urgency. "Caleb is a renown humanitarian, but, over the years, I've noticed something about him that makes me suspicious of his true nature."

"The way he flared up at Danica during dinner gave me a hint of his dark side," Kenzie admitted.

"Yet, you brought me here to meet him!" I accused.

"It was when I thought that you were a mutt," he apologetically admitted. "Watered down women don't get the best of treatment from their mates in general. He seemed to be the better of the choices. Had I realized that you
were of pure lineage, I'd have never made the introduction."

"And Noah wouldn't have used me for sex and then dumped me," I hissed. "Is that what you're telling me?"

"It sounds terrible when you say it like that, but, yes," he replied. "Had Noah realized that you weren't watered down, he would have behaved differently."

"Is that supposed to make me want to go rushing back to him?" I asked with full resentment.

"Do you think that Caleb would have wanted you if you were truly not pure?" he defensively asked. "When I called to tell him that I was bringing you to meet him, I didn't mention it to him in hopes that he'd see you for the wonderful woman that you are and overlook what my dumbass brother couldn't. Instead, he saw the magic veil around you right away."

"He has the gift like me," I said.

"Which, Noah does not," Kenzie reminded me. "After listening to their dinner talk and witnessing Danica's reaction when she thought an inferior mutt was going to mate with her cousin, I can understand why both Noah and Caleb would be cautious of who they mated with."

"It's unfair to overlook the fact that Caleb made a decision knowing your true lineage and Noah did not," Oscar argued.

"The old crone said that I was born to be a queen," I said with angst. "From where I stand, I'm nothing but chattel to be fought over."

Oscar vigorously shook his head.

"That's not true," he said. "I can see where you might feel that because you're unfamiliar with our ways. The fact of the matter is that if the old crone said that you are to be a queen, then you need to think long and hard about who you mate with because, once your lineage is learned by the masses, they'll expect you to be paired off with royalty. To do otherwise would be just as bad as it would be for a pack leader to mate with a watered down female."

"Is Caleb royalty?" Kenzie asked.

"He is, but of a lesser station than Noah," he replied.

Kenzie looked at me with raised brow.

"No," I blurted out. "I won't go back to

22

Noah after what he did. I don't care how much pressure his pack puts on him. I refuse to accept being treated like that." Then, as an afterthought I vehemently said, "If either of you tell him the truth about me, I won't forgive you. Let him think that Caleb did what he could not. It serves him right."

"Danica might spill the beans," Kenzie offered.

"I doubt that," I replied. "You heard what Caleb said about the fact that I'd be competition for her with Noah. She's already struggling to get him to mate with her. I can't imagine she'd want him to know about me in case Caleb's right about Noah's feelings."

"He is," Oscar quickly interjected.

"Humph," I huffed. "You couldn't prove it by me."

"My brother can be an ass at times," Oscar mumbled.

"If you don't go back to Noah's house, we'll be forced to leave you hear," Kenzie lamented. "I don't like it. Something doesn't feel right. I wish you'd forgive Noah and give him another chance."

When I pursed my lips together and stubbornly shook my head she heaved a sigh of resignation. Giving me a long, worried hug good-bye, she slid into the passenger's seat of the SUV and waved good-bye to me as they drove out of the sanctuary's compound.

I stood watching until their vehicle disappeared before realizing just how alone and nervous I truly felt.

36

The guest room where I was placed in the big house was adjacent to Caleb's. In fact, there was a concealed door that allowed him to enter without going into the hallway. This wasn't something that I was aware of until I heard it open a few hours after I'd gone to bed.

I was in that zen state of not being fully awake, yet not quite into a deep sleep when I heard the creaking of the door. My mind was aware of it, but my body remained unwilling to respond as I peacefully lay beneath the damask coverlet that adorned the bed.

The wherewithal to react finally hit me when I felt the cool air on my nakedness as the covers were pulled away from me. Sitting up, I quickly turned on the light while pulling the top sheet up high enough to cover my bare breasts.

I rarely slept in the nude, but since I'd arrived with the intention of an afternoon visit and not a lengthy stay, I had no night clothes to wear. I could have remained in my bra and panties, but I'd opted to rinse them out so that they'd be fresh for the following morning. Had I realized that Caleb was going to sneak into my room to invade my sleep, I would have done things differently.

"My, but you're a beauty," he said as he forced my arms down so that he could better see my breasts. "I suspected as much, but it's gratifying to know it's fact. Werewolves don't simply admire a body for the pleasure it will give. We also take into consideration its ability to breed and support strong offspring. You are not only beautiful to look at, but your body looks strong and healthy."

"You need to leave," I harshly ordered.

He grinned as he pushed me back onto the pillow and positioned himself astride over my torso.

"I think I'll stay for a bit longer and get to know my future mate," he said with what I interpreted as a sinister chuckle.

"I don't want this," I said as he lowered his face so close to mine that the heat of his breath caressed my cheeks.

"That's not the impression I got downstairs when I kissed you," he argued. "Admit it, Lisa, we're meant to be together. You felt it just as much as I did."

"I want you to leave," I argued. "Leave,

or I'll scream."

"Just who do you think will come to your aid?" he asked with amusement. Then, with a more serious tone, he added, "I barely know Noah, but I suspect he's had a taste of you. Your cape reeked of his scent. Not only did Danica hint to it, but I got a glimpse of it from your psyche. You either had sex with him or want to have sex with him. Either way, I'm here to wipe that out of your aura."

"How?" I nervously asked.

"You know how," he grumbled as he lowered his lips to mine.

Unlike earlier in the night, his kiss didn't excite me and make me desire more. It frightened me and made me want him to leave and never come back. The situation was far too reminiscent of my being raped by the lake for my liking.

Feeling panicked, I attempted to push him away so that I could beg him to stop and leave, but he held me in a vice grip while keeping his lips planted firmly on mine. As his tongue explored the cavity of my mouth, I noticed a faint rosemary and mint taste that caused a tingling sensation. It began in my mouth, but eventually spread all the way to my fingers and toes.

The body can be a fickle thing. At least mine can. I cursed it inwardly when his strong hand slid between the apex of my thighs and I slowly responded to the teasing of my womanhood. My intense panic was replaced by extreme sexual desire. It became so potent that I found my arms wrapped around his neck and my hips bucking with need.

Never in my life had I behaved in such a way in the bedroom, yet I felt no shame in it. I simply felt the need to have more and more sexual gratification.

It was then that he stopped kissing me so that he could make good use of his mouth on my breasts.

I arched my back to give him greater access to breasts that were swollen with desire. He moaned his pleasure with each response that I made as he slowly discovered what to do to me to get the most intense reaction.

When he finally drove his powerful manhood deep inside of me, I climaxed almost immediately.

All thoughts of Noah flew out of my mind as I focused on the pleasure of his touch. It was nothing like I envisioned a woman should experience with a man she had no feelings for. What occurred between Caleb and me was far from the love making that I'd reveled in with Noah. It was more of an animalistic type of eroticism that erased all sensibility of thought other than the intense desire to be sexually satiated. Then, I'd known Noah long enough to fall in love with him before we shared bodies. I'd only just met Caleb a few hours earlier. It stood to reason that I'd feel only lust instead of love. The lust was almost too intense, though. I suspected that I'd go mad if it continued much longer.

Digging my fingers deep into his buttocks, I methodically slammed my hips against his as I tried to draw him deep inside of me. It was an action that was new to me, but I gave it or the loud slapping sound that it made throughout the room little consideration. My only thought, my only desire was to meld with him. To become one. The fact that I couldn't manage it was frustrating.

"I want you deep inside of me. I need all of you in me," I panted.

"I'm going to give you my seed and bite you at the same time," he murmured. "Then, you're mine."

Since Noah had already explained that werewolves couldn't pass on an STD, that fear was nil, but there was still the matter of pregnancy. Unfortunately, not only did I not care about anything other than being sexually satiated, but before I could get my wits about me and respond, he did just as he'd declared he would do.

The heat of his seed pouring into me made my womanhood possessively wrap around his swollen rod while my body shuddered with erotic delight. I'd expected to suffer from the bite, but my sexual arousal heightened to the extent of overshadowing any pain.

He'd extended his wolf fangs and bit me in the neck, but it wasn't enough. I felt the need for a deeper connection. I wanted him to bite me again and again. When I breathily declared this to him, he chuckled and drove his fangs just a bit deeper into my flesh. I could feel him sucking on my blood. Instead of frightening me, it aroused me even more.

When he finally released my neck, I gasped and said, "More. Bite me more."

"As you wish," he said with obvious satisfaction.

"Everywhere," I said with a hint of desperation. "I feel like I need you to possess every inch of me."

He held his face above mine for a brief moment as he studied my face before taking my nipple into his mouth and sinking his fangs around it. It was painful at first, but, as his tongue teased the tip of my nipple, the pain turned to sheer erotic delight. When he moved to the next breast, I was ready and eager for what I knew would happen.

The fact that his strong fingers were working their magic on my sensitive nub intensified the experience.

I arched my back and moaned my

pleasure as I held his head in place to prevent him from pulling back before I was ready.

Reaching up, he gently removed my trembling hands from his head and slowly pulled his fangs from my flesh. I felt him lick the blood from the puncture wounds that enveloped my swollen areola before he gently parted my legs and move his head so that his mouth was over my womanhood. I thought that he was going to pierce me there next and, to be honest, I was a tad worried about the pain that it might cause. Instead, he slid his fingers deep inside of me and attacked my sensitive nub with his strong tongue until I was practically mad with pleasure.

I wrapped my legs around his neck as I lost myself in the delights of his ministrations. I was so involved with my own pleasure that I didn't realize that as soon as I climaxed, he moved to drive his fangs deep into my inner thigh just below my womanhood until I felt his hands holding my leg steady in a vice-like grip.

Whether it was because I'd achieved that sexual release that I'd been begging for or if it was the location of the bite, I wasn't sure, but this time, the pain was anything but pleasant. I called out for him to stop as I tried to twist free, but he held firm. In fact, instead of releasing the pressure, he drove his fangs even deeper. The sound of him sucking at my blood echoed through my head. I felt a small surge of relief when he finally pulled his fangs from the meat of my leg, but it was short lived as he immediately did the same thing to my other thigh.

My thoughts went to vampirism as I felt him suck the blood from me. It was then that I realized that he'd consumed a good deal of it when all was said and done. Since I didn't know much about werewolves, I wasn't sure if that was a common thing. After all, perhaps it wasn't just vampires who drank blood. Perhaps it was something that werewolves did on a lesser scale. I just didn't know.

As he'd done with my breast, when he removed his fangs from my flesh, he licked the blood from the wound.

As he stretched out on the bed beside me and pulled me into his arms, I realized that he was still fully clothed. Too exhausted to be concerned over it, I allowed my body to drift off into blissful nothingness.

37

When I awoke, I was surprised to discover that I'd slept through the majority of the day. To add to my confusion, I felt weak and exhausted.

I was about to climb out of bed and find the nearest bathroom when the door to my bedroom opened and the cook entered with a food tray.

"Good. You're awake," he said with a deep, baritone voice that didn't match his short, stocky stature. "I've brought you some broth. You're to drink it all up."

Extremely self-conscious of my nakedness, I held the sheet tight to my collarbone as I said, "I need to go to the bathroom."

His tone was matter-of-fact as he said, "There's a bedpan under the bed."

"What?" I said with surprise. "I'm to use a bedpan? Why can't I just use the bathroom?"

"I was given instructions to keep you in the room no matter what," he explained.

Although I was livid to hear such a thing, I kept focused on the matter at hand. I needed to empty my bladder and I had no intention of using a bed pan when there was a perfectly good bathroom just outside my bedroom door.

"I'm not using a bedpan. There's a bathroom just out in the hall. I'm using that," I insistently said.

He shrugged as he set the tray down on a nearby side table and grumbled, "Suit yourself, but I'll have to take you."

"I don't need you to escort me," I declared with obvious indignation. "I know where it is. I used it last night to prepare for bed."

I could have sworn that I detected a glint of amusement in his beady eyes when he asked, "Have you tried to walk yet?"

"Excuse me?" I said with emphasis.

"Have you tried to walk yet," he said with equal emphasis. "It's a simple enough question."

"What kind of a question is that?" I spat.

When I'd first set eyes on the cook, I'd experienced mixed emotions, but I'd chalked it up to him being a part of a situation that was as abnormal as they come. At that moment, I realized that it was more than that. There was something dark and sleazy about this ugly little man.

He arrogantly folded his arms over his chest and said, "Try it."

"I would, but I'm naked," I replied without thinking.

"I've already seen all that you have to offer," he informed me. When I gasped with disbelief, he added, "I'm the one who cleaned you up after he was done with you."

Ignoring the implications of his poor choice of words, I quickly peeked beneath the sheet to investigate his claim. Sure enough, there were bandages covering my swollen nipples and over the wounds on my inner thighs. I reached for the area of my neck where he'd bitten and it too was bandaged.

"You've got great tits," he informed me. "They're bigger and fuller than you'd expect to find on someone so small, but they don't look out of place. I checked inside you. You're nice and snug. You haven't born any children yet, have you? I told the boss that I was a little worried about that. Your hips are a bit narrow, but he seems to think you'll do fine."

I practically choked on the air that I sucked in as I listened with horror.

"You're disgusting," I bellowed. "Get out!"

He displayed crooked, yellowed teeth as he tossed his head back with full bellied laughter before exiting the room. I waited to make sure that he was gone before climbing out of bed. To my dismay, my legs gave way and I fell to the floor. Confused, I held onto the bed's footboard as I struggled to stand, but to no avail. My legs were completely useless. I could only assume that it had to do with the intense, painful bites that he'd given me.

Tears of frustration slid down my cheeks as I reached beneath the bed for the bedpan. It took some maneuvering to secure it beneath me. After relieving myself, I was horrified when I realized that I ran the risk of tipping it over and having its contents spill onto the thick Persian carpet that adorned the gleaming hardwood floor if I didn't get help. Frustrated and mortified, I shouted for the creepy cook to return.

He must have been waiting just outside the door because I'd barely called for him before he was entering the room while uttering a satisfied chuckle.

"Put your arms around my neck," he said as he bent so low that his lips were parallel with my exposed nipples.

Left with no options, I did as he asked. I could feel the heat of his breath graze a nipple and worried that he'd try to place his lips on it. To my relief, he simply pulled me to my feet. We stood still for a moment before he backed away from the bedpan. Grabbing the tissue box, he pulled out a few tissues and reached between my legs.

"What are you doing?" I gasped.

"You need to be wiped," he explained with just a bit too much pleasure. "Since your hands are busy, I'll do the honors."

I did my best to remain stoic and deny him the satisfaction of knowing how mortified I was that he was wiping the excess pee from me. His movements were far too slow and deliberate for my liking, yet I couldn't say that he was doing anything other than wiping me clean. So, I said nothing. I simply closed my eyes and grit my teeth together while I waited for my moment of humiliation to cease.

When he was finished, he set me back onto the bed and tossed the sheet over me.

"I want you to drink all of this broth," he ordered as he pulled the table close to the bed. "If you want to walk again, you'll do it."

"What's happened to my legs?" I meekly asked.

He studied me for a moment before asking, "Didn't he tell you beforehand?" When I slowly shook my head, he heaved a sigh and added, "It's part of the transitional ritual. It will help you in the long run with your turning. It's a gradual and less painful way of doing it."

"Turning?" I gasped.

"You are a pure werewolf," he said with an attitude that suggested he shouldn't have to remind me of such things, "so the process will be a lot easier than if you weren't."

"He's turning me?" I cried. "I didn't ask to be turned. I don't want to be turned."

The ugly little man looked at me with a mixture of surprise and disdain as he asked, "How do you expect to bear healthy werewolf children if you don't turn beforehand? Your genes must be activated." When I gave no reply, he grabbed the bedpan and headed for the door. Stopping with his hand on the doorknob, he turned and said, "Be thankful that he cares enough about you to do it this way instead of letting the process take place from start to finish during the full moon. Even for someone who's pure like you, it can be an excruciating process for the first few times."

"I can't believe this is happening," I moaned as I sank into the pillow.

"Heed my warning and drink that broth if you want to use those legs again," he ordered as he left the room.

38

I hadn't eaten since the dinner party the night before, so the spicy broth hit the spot.

It occurred to me to question its contents, but, then, I thought better of it. What did it matter? I didn't like being handicapped in such a way. It actually brought forth hints of the claustrophobia that I suffered from. As the creepy cook so adamantly insisted; if I wanted to use my legs, I'd have to drink the broth and I definitely wanted to use my legs again.

I found the fact that this broth had such crazy healing properties puzzling since it tasted like a simple Asian beef broth to me. Since I knew so little about werewolves and their ways, I accepted that it had some type of property that would renew my ability to function normally and drank every last drop.

I didn't get a chance to test out the results of the broth before Caleb returned to my room. I'd fallen into a deep, dreamless sleep almost immediately after consuming it.

When I awoke, it was well after midnight and he was climbing into bed beside me.

"No," I sleepily groaned into the pillow as I turned so that my back was facing him. "Last night was a mistake. I don't behave like that with men I've just met. In fact, I don't behave like that with men I've known for a while. It wasn't like me. I don't know why I did it, but I won't do it again. No more."

He gently rubbed his work calloused palm over the smooth flesh of my shoulder blades while saying in a soft voice, "I have begun the process of your shift, my dear. It would not bode well for you to stop now."

"By biting me while having kinky sex?" I accusingly bellowed into the down filled fabric. "I never said that I wanted to turn into a werewolf each month. You shouldn't have done that."

"One way or another, you'll have to turn," he said with mild impatience. "If I don't take you for a mate, someone else will. Believe me when I tell you that they won't be as considerate about easing your shifting process as I am. They'll let it all happen under the full moon within a matter of hours. Bones will break, muscles will tear, and you'll feel like you're going to die before it's over." He waited for a brief moment before adding, "As for the kinky sex, arousal and pleasure release a hormone that helps to

257

ease the intensity of the pain of the venom entering the body. I can do it without the sex, but you'd wish I hadn't."

I sat up and turned to face him.

"I tried to walk today and couldn't," I spat. "I had to have that ugly werewolf cook's help just to go pee."

He smirked, but said nothing.

"You think that's funny?" I indignantly bellowed. "I was naked, you know. I don't know about your customs, but I was raised to value my dignity just a little bit more than I'm being allowed."

"I'm sorry," he hurriedly said. "I don't think that's funny at all. I was
responding to the term you used for Philip. He's not a werewolf. Although, I'll agree that he's a bit ugly."

"He's not?" I said with surprise. "Why is he here with you and privy to it all if he's not one of you?"

"Why is Kenzie with Oscar?" he defensively replied.

"They're in love," I spat. "Do you love Philip? Is that it?"

He gave me a look of mild offense and impatience, but said nothing in response to my accusation. I got the impression that he was remaining silent while he focused on keeping his anger in check.

"He'd like to be turned, but he carries no gene that's strong enough," he finally offered. "Philip's ancestors mixed too many times with humans. His gene is too weak to sustain him in a turn. His genetics are ninety-five percent human. He would surely die."

"I thought that any hint of werewolf gene would be enough," I mused with thoughtfulness.

He slowly shook his head.

"Would that it be true, but it's not," he explained. "The gene has to be one-third equal to the human genes or stronger. If not, the person trying to shift runs the risk of perishing during the process."

"If shifting is that bad, why do it?" I asked.

He laid back against the pillow with his hands behind his head.

Looking at the ceiling as if he was inspecting it, he said, "First of all, it's not that bad if it's done correctly. If the body is slowly acclimated to the venom before the first turn, it's a fairly easy shift. Once the first shift is over and the body knows what to do, it will remember. After a while, it actually feels so good to shift that you begin to crave it."

"I can't imagine craving something like that," I scoffed.

He flashed me one of his sexy grins as he chuckled and said, "We'll see."

"I take it that you introduced your

venom to my body when you bit me," I observed.

He nodded as he said, "I placed it in your breasts and legs to assist you not only with the turn, but to make it so that you will bear strong, healthy children."

"How is putting venom in my breasts or legs going to do that?" I asked with genuine curiosity. "Why not just bite me in a main vein and get it into my bloodstream?"

"It goes into your blood and spreads, but when it is placed in specific locations, it will make them more potent as well. It's my intention to introduce my venom into other parts of your body. I just didn't want to do it all at once. It can be too much if it's not done gradually," he said. "The venom in your breast will promote better milk for the baby. Your leg muscles will be stronger because they have my venom in their fibers along with your own. It's kind of like souping up a racing machine. I'm making you more of what you already are. Also, because my venom is in you, it will help to ease the shifting process. It might not even be difficult. I know it will definitely be much easier than if I did nothing to aid you."

"You left it up to that creepy cook to clean me up," I accusingly said. "Why would you do that? He saw everything I had to offer."

"I'm sorry," he said with what sounded

genuine. "I was called out on an emergency in confines for the wild. The wolf had some sort of seizure. I didn't want to risk you bleeding out. I had no choice but ask for help. He's the only one I trust with you. He's gay, you know."

"No, I didn't know," I replied as I thought back on my accusation of Caleb and Philip being in love with regret. Then, changing the subject, I pouted, "I'm not taking birth control. You may have gotten me pregnant last night."

"I certainly hope so," he enthusiastically said as he rolled onto his side to face me. "It was my intention."

"We aren't a couple," I complained. "That was pretty presumptuous of you."

He raised a brow with surprise as he asked, "Do you have someone else in mind?"

I did, but I wasn't about to admit it to him. As angry and disappointed as I was with Noah, I couldn't shake the feelings that I had for him. In the recesses of my being, I still had hope that he'd come to love me like I did him. I was even tempted to take back my orders from Oscar and Kenzie about keeping my heritage from him.

I'd given their argument a good deal of consideration and they were right. Caleb made his offer to me because he knew my lineage. Of course, he didn't have sex with me and then ignore me, but perhaps Noah only did that to protect me from Danica's wrath. After being around that evil she-wolf enough to see how truly volatile she could be and hearing Caleb and Oscar discuss the stress of being a pack leader, my anger with Noah had lessened. It hadn't gone away completely, but it was far less intense to the extent that I was actually sympathetic toward his position.

It was at that moment that it struck me. I'd had sex with Noah just the day before I'd had sex with Caleb. Noah had also left his seed in me, yet it never crossed my mind to worry that he may have impregnated me. Now that the concern was a real one, I also had to worry about who the father might be. Worse yet... if the father was Noah, would Caleb's venom help or hurt the baby?

I needed to speak to someone about this concern, but I just didn't know who.

"Don't look so worried," he murmured as he pulled me with such force beneath him that it was impossible to prevent it. "I'll finish depositing my venom tonight. There's just a few more places that need it to make you as strong as you can possibly be."

Worried about what more venom might do to a child that belonged to Noah, I tried to fight him off. All I managed to do was to excite him all the more.

"I like it when you show me your spitfire side," he cooed as he kissed the well of my neck. "I can't wait to see what you're like as a wolf."

39

I was disgusted both with myself and with Caleb. He'd managed to subdue my body and get the response from it that he wanted through sex while he left his venom inside me night after night. Week after week. Surprisingly, unlike with Noah, the more time I spent with him, the less I liked him. By the time the moon's cycle had reached the brink of another full moon, I could say that I actually hated him.

Unlike when I awoke after the first venom installment, I not only could use my legs, but they were so full of energy that it was almost too much. I needed to walk some of it off, but since Caleb was afraid that I'd run away, I still wasn't allowed to leave the room.

As I paced the floor with my new and improved legs, I found that I was moving with the ease and grace that reminded me of a caged panther I'd admired in a zoo when I was younger. Approaching the window just in time to see Kenzie pulling into the driveway, I immediately rushed to the door to go downstairs and greet her, only to discover that it was locked. Feeling trapped and panicked, I struggled to think on what to do.

Kenzie was getting back into her SUV when I finally returned to the window. Desperate to get her attention and help, I clumsily fumbled with the window lock. I was about to give up and smash the windowpane when the lock gave way and I was able to raise the window far enough for me to hang out of it.

My friend was famous for driving with her radio blasting, so I questioned if the frantic waiving of my arms while I shouted her name would be enough to penetrate the music that I was certain she had playing.

Fortunately, it did.

Stopping the vehicle, she hopped out and bellowed, "What are you doing? I thought that you were napping!"

Mindless of who was listening, I called out, "I'm their prisoner. Please, get me out of here."

With a look of shocked surprise, she quickly scoped the grounds before asking in a more normal tone, but still one that I could hear, "Are you serious?"

"I couldn't be more so," I replied. "He's pumped me full of his venom and intends to have me turn during the next full moon."

"That's in two days," she thoughtfully said.

"I didn't give him permission to do that," I vehemently complained. "I never said that I wanted to turn into a werewolf. I also never actually agreed to mate with him. He's forceful and won't take no for an answer. He's also trying to impregnate me. You need to get me out of here."

The ugly fat cook named Philip bound out onto the porch. Whatever he said to her, it was said so that I couldn't be privy to it. With a look of sadness, she peered up at me before blowing me a kiss and getting back into her SUV.

Deflated, shocked, disappointed, and furious, I watched my friend and only hope of being free of my nightmare drive away.

Wiping at the tears that flowed freely down my cheeks, I paced the room once more. I needed to walk off the excess energy before I hurt someone or myself.

With no television, radio, or book to occupy my time, there was little else to do other than sleep or pace the room. When the pacing finally gave me a semblance of relief from the pent up energy, I flopped onto the bed and closed my eyes.

I'd almost drifted into a light sleep when I heard the lock on the door turn. Quickly sitting up, I waited to see if it was going to be the ugly cook or Caleb paying me a visit.

It was neither.

"What is this nonsense you're spreading?" Danica snipped as she sauntered into the room like the Queen of Sheba. "Really, Lisa. Hanging out of the window screaming that you're being held prisoner? Can you be more dramatic?"

"Or, truthful?" I replied.

My body coiled into defense mode as she hurried toward me with a look of vengeance in her eyes and determination in her movements

"Caleb would never hold you here against your will, you lying bitch!" she snarled. "You're just trying to do what? Play on Noah's sympathies? Is that it? Were you hoping your friend would go running to Noah and beg him to rescue you? Huh?" Her face was a mere inch or two from mine. Her breath felt hot on my face as I focused on her eyes as a red halo circled the irises while she said between clenched teeth, "What do you think he'll do when he finds out it's all a lie?" Spinning on her heels, her long, coarse hair slapped my face as she turned her back to me and stomped toward the door. "You can't have them all, Lisa. You've got Caleb. Be content with that. Noah's mine."

"Caleb isn't who you think he is," I stammered. "I don't want him."

She stopped with her hand on the

doorknob and slowly turned her head to give me a look that was so evil it made me shudder.

"He's exactly who I think he is, and you'd better want him because I won't let you have Noah. I'll kill you first. You should thank your lucky stars that you caught Caleb's eye. After all, he's a pack leader and there aren't a lot of them. Life could be so much worse with one of the lower members of the pack," she said. Then, with a sly grin, she added, "If I had my way, I'd mate you to one of the dregs. It would serve you right."

"I don't want to be mated. Nor do I want to become a werewolf," I blurted out. "I just want to be left alone."

She studied me for a brief moment before opening the door. As she slid through the opening, she called out, "Remember what I said. Noah belongs to me."

I sank onto the edge of the bed. Had the whole world gone mad? Was there no escape from this nightmare? The anger and hate that I felt for Danica intensified as her words rolled around in my head. Thank my lucky stars? What lucky stars? As far as I could tell, I'd had no luck of late.

I sat in silence while staring at nothing in particular until sunset. Philip silently entered with my tray of food and, then, quickly slipped out of the room. When he returned an hour later to find it untouched, he heavily scolded me before returning it to the kitchen.

When Caleb entered a few minutes later, I heaved a sigh of resignation. I was his prisoner and, from where I stood, his sex toy. I could either fight it and suffer or go along with it and possibly come through with a little less pain that I'd been experiencing. I was so tired of fighting. I just couldn't do it anymore. Besides, it didn't do much to help the situation, other than tire me out and leave me with a few bruises now and then.

His look of surprise was followed by a broad smile when he saw me stand and robotically disrobe.

"Now, that's how I like to be greeted," he enthusiastically said. "It certainly took you long enough."

Opening his pants to exposed his aroused manhood, he rushed toward me like a dog in heat.

40

There were still a matter of hours before the full moon would rise and I already felt terrible. In fact, the sensations in my body were so strange and awful that I couldn't even accurately describe them to anyone if I tried. Every inch of me twitched and ached, from my bones to my muscles.

Since I'd never experienced this before, I suspected that it had to do with the fact that I had Caleb's venom inside of me. I would have confirmed it with him, but he was nowhere to be found. After I'd submitted so willingly to him a few nights earlier, he'd not returned. It was almost as if he'd lost interest after a successful conquest of my body.

Since I'd arrived almost a week earlier, I'd not been allowed out of my room. The only faces I'd seen were Caleb, Philip, and Danica. Kenzie returned several times over the course of the few days, but was unsuccessful in getting near me. It was pure torture to see her trying to gain entry to the house, only to be turned away. I was both confused and curious as to why Oscar wasn't with her during her attempts. After conquering the hurt that I felt over his not rescuing me, I thought long and hard and came to the conclusion that it was because he wasn't allowed to go against a pack leader, even if the leader belonged to a different pack. Since I wasn't able to speak with Kenzie, I didn't know for sure, but, since he unwillingly left me there because Caleb was a pack leader and he wasn't, it made sense that he wouldn't attempt to rescue me.

Oh how I wished I knew whether they'd gone against my wishes and told Noah that I was being held prisoner. If so, was he also simply leaving me to my fate? Since he believed me to be a mutt, he probably was.

The sun was just beginning to set over the treetops when I felt a piercing pain in my abdomen. It came on so fast and so strong that I doubled over. I wrapped my arms around my stomach and hugged it as if it would, somehow, make it all better.

My vision got progressively blurred as the pain increased. By the time Philip entered the room with a light meal for me, I was covered with perspiration from the agony and could barely make out his form.

"What's going on?" he bellowed as he

dropped the food tray on the bedside table and rushed to investigate my condition. Pulling my legs open, he emitted a sound that sounded more like a growl than a groan as he declared, "You're bleeding, heavily. Are you miscarrying?"

"I... I don't know," I managed to choke out as I buried my face into the pillow. "Oh damn! It feels like someone's stabbing me in the gut."

"You're miscarrying," he said with a voice that was now steady and firm. "I've seen it happen just before a shift a few times, but the baby didn't belong to the mate. The venom deposited in the woman wasn't compatible with the fetus and it aborted. This shouldn't be happening with you."

"Well, it is," I snapped as I rolled onto my back. "I need to go to the hospital."

"Wait here," he said as he rushed to the door. "I'll get help."

Even in the middle of all of my suffering, I couldn't help note the irony of his statement. Wait here? I couldn't even straighten my body. Just where did he expect me to wander off to?

I had no idea how long I lay in agony while I lamented over the fact that I was obviously losing Noah's baby before Danica's shrill voice permeated the room.

"Get her off the bed!" she bellowed.

"She's bleeding all over the place. She's going to ruin the mattress."

"No," I groaned with dismay.

Danica was far from what I'd consider help. I had no doubt that, if left up to her, I'd be allowed to bleed to death while she sat and watched while sipping on a glass of expensive wine.

"Look at this mess," she snarled. "Leave it to you to miscarriage Caleb's child. You couldn't even carry it a few weeks! He's a fool to think you'd make a good mate."

I was tempted to tell her that I suspected the child to have been Noah's and not Caleb's, but I thought better of it. From the way she was behaving, I didn't believe she was aware that I'd actually done more than share his bed while he guarded me. Something in my gut told me that sharing that bit of information with her could prove lethal.

So, I said nothing.

"We'll have to get her cleaned up before Caleb returns," she hissed as she yanked at my panties to get them off me.

I'd foregone wearing my clothes and simply stuck to my bra and panties when I realized that I wasn't going to be let out of the room and they'd sealed the windows. The closeness of the room made it difficult to breathe and clothes simply added to my feeling of being closed in.

"It's just my period," I finally moaned as I made a feeble attempt to kick Danica away from me. "I don't need you to do that. I'm capable of cleaning myself up."

"Don't try to fool me," she said with disdain. "I've seen plenty of miscarriages by mutts. Are you sure you're not one of them?"

"Go away," I spat as I kicked her hard in the stomach.

I smiled with satisfaction as the sound of a disgruntled grunt that was emphasized by air being forced out of her by my kick reached my ears.

"Bitch!" she choked out.

Undeterred by her anger, I rolled off the bed, landing on my knees on the floor next to it.

"I'll be damned if I'll let you strip me. Get out of here. I can take care of this myself!" I bellowed. Seething from the inside out, my angry eyes darted from her to Philip and then back to her again. When neither of them moved, I bellowed with greater emphasis, "Get out!"

Philip was quick to obey my last outburst, but Danica merely sauntered at an excruciatingly slow pace toward the door. When she finally reached it, she stopped to study me.

"The moon will rise soon and you'll begin your first shift," she said with smug

satisfaction. "It was my intention to run with Noah, but I might just
stick around to watch. I'm sure it will be quite a show."

"Get out!" I vehemently screamed as I rose to my feet.

Whether she saw the intent to kill in my eyes or had simply had her fill of annoying me, I wasn't sure, but she left without another word.

The cramping had dulled to a tolerable level. I tried the door and found it open, so I rushed to the bathroom to wash up. There was no time to waste. Danica's final taunt had reminded me that I was racing against the clock.

41

Caleb waited until an hour before the moon was full to come to my room. Furious at being ignored by him for days, I snarled as he entered.

"You're in the process of shifting, I see," he said with a smug smile as he lowered himself into the room's only easy chair that was located in the far corner. Resting his elbows on its thickly padded arms, he touched the tips of his fingers together, tapping his index fingers lightly as he spoke. "I understand you miscarried. I suspected as much."

I went to respond to him, but found that my voice didn't want to cooperate. I was shocked at how foreign it sounded to me when I finally managed to eke out, "What?"

"I lied, you see," he said as he sat forward. "It's true that putting venom into your system promoted your shift, but I didn't need to put as much as I did. One small bite would have been sufficient. I could smell Noah Spears' scent on your body that first night and I knew that he'd impregnated you. I didn't put that much of my venom in you to make you bear stronger children for us. I put it in you to kill his child. I'll be damned if I'll start a relationship with another man's child in your belly. The added strength you feel is simply a by-product of the process." I felt a sudden, overwhelming hatred for him that exceeded anything I'd felt before. When I growled and glowered in an effort to let him know exactly how I was feeling, he added, "Had it been my child, you would have been fine. I just knew it wasn't my offspring in your belly." Heaving a sigh, he stood and said, "Something had to be done. We need to start out right. Now, we can have our own children with no questions about genetics. That's everything in the werewolf kingdom, you know. Genetics, that is."

For the first time since I'd met him he looked ugly to me. Just like his cousin, Danica, it started on the inside and permeated to the surface. I didn't know why I hadn't seen it from the start. The fact that his smile never reached his eyes should have clued me in. Or, perhaps Danica being his family would have been a good clue as well. Evil was probably part of their genetic makeup.

I thought about how compassionate Oscar was and how caring and gentle Noah had been right up until he turned his back on me after we'd had beautiful sex. Again, I wondered how he'd have behaved had Danica not paid him a visit at that time.

All thoughts of anything but survival fled my mind when a sudden surge of painful energy permeated my body.

Seeing me writhe in agony, Caleb stood up and announced that it was time to take me outside so that I could complete my shift while surrounded by nature. His lack of empathy was shocking as he grabbed my hand and practically dragged me down the stairs and out of the house.

I did my best to keep up with him and, by some miracle, managed not to lose my footing. Such was his apathy for my condition that I had no doubt that, had I fallen, he would have kept going and simply dragged me along.

We entered a circle of werewolves who had already either begun their shift or completed it. None of them seemed to suffer the experience. In fact, they made their transition quickly and quietly.

I, on the other hand, howled with agony as I fell to the ground. Caleb quickly pulled my undergarments off me. I was mentally mortified over the fact that I was naked in front of a group of strangers, but I seemed to be the only one who was aware of it. Or, who cared. All conversation and anticipation was on how long it would take for me to shift and how painful it would be for me.

I seethed inside as I listened to Caleb explain to the onlookers that he'd deposited a vast amount of his venom into my system and that he hoped it didn't impair my shift. The viciousness of his actions hit home at that moment. When he announced that he'd decided to take me as a mate upon seeing me but his decision was even more solidified when he discovered that I was royalty, I wanted to hurt him.

Pain permeated my body and I felt feverish. My mind cried out for help from someone, anyone, but my mouth and vocal cords couldn't coordinate. All I managed to get past my lips was a long, low moan as I fell onto my knees and hands in an instinctive move of preparation for what was to come.

My mouth hurt like someone was sticking needles into my gums and my nose burned. I could feel my face distort. It surprised me because it felt as if I was literally developing the face of a wolf, like Snow. When I'd seen Noah and Oscar shift, they'd still resembled men in many ways. I got the impression that wasn't going to happen with me. I wanted to ask why, but I couldn't.

The answer came from someone in the crowd once I'd fully turned into a real live wolf.

"Will you look at that? She's pure wolf," someone called from behind me. "You must have really peppered her with your venom, Caleb."

"I might have gone a bit overboard," Caleb admitted, "but it will wear off after she shifts a few times."

"I thought I'd be attending a mating ceremony. How are you going to mate with her when she's in full canine form?" someone else asked.

My head whirled around upon hearing that question. Was that why there were so many of them circled around me? Had they come to see me mated to Caleb?

It was bad enough that he'd taken it upon himself to make sure that I shifted and miscarried. The fact that he also planned on mating with me no matter how I felt about it was simply too much.

I'd had all I could handle when I heard my would be intended announce that he'd need some help in subduing me so that he could solidify the mating ceremony by mounting me.

Mount me? It sounded barbaric and offensive to my ears.

Without a moment's thought or hesitation, I sprang to life.

I hoped that my threatening snarl was as effective as Snow's had been as I bounded out of the circle and into the woods. It certainly took them by surprise, if only for a moment.

Because they hadn't expected me to behave in such a way, I had just
enough of the element of surprise on my side to give me an adequate head start before they set out to find me.

My mind felt muddled. I was just barely aware of who I was, but that identity of self was fading fast.

My senses were heightened beyond my wildest imagination and I could feel the difference in my body composition. I had to fight the urge to hunt the little forest creatures that scurried about as I struggled to remember that I was actually human and had a pack of werewolves chasing after me.

I felt incredibly powerful by the unbelievable amount of adrenaline that permeated every muscle as I raced in the direction that I thought would take me to Noah's cabin.

I had no idea why I wanted to go there. It wasn't as if I'd find solace or safety. Yet, I was driven to get there as fast as my four legs would take me.

The faint sound of Caleb's pack in the distance only served to push me onward with even more power than I thought possible.

My heart hammered at my chest and my lungs steadily pumped air in and out of them as I lept over fallen trees and bounded

281

over clusters of small boulders. All the while, my focus remained on getting to that cabin.

My vision was remarkably accurate in the darkness. This came in handy as my eyes searched the forest for the ancient rustic dwelling. I'd just spotted it in the distance when Snow lept in front of me.

Stopping in my tracks, I snarled a warning. My thoughts struggled with whether I should consider him friend or foe. After all, he'd killed a man to save me from rape and capture, yet, he didn't seem to be all that eager to do much of anything for me at that moment save clamp his powerful fangs into my throat.

With each of us emitting our own threatening snarls, we slowly circled each other. I got the impression that he didn't immediately attack because he was confused over what to do. There was a spark of recognition in his eyes as he sniffed the air between snarls.

Did he recognize my scent? Was it still similar to when I was human?

I had no idea.

42

Noah's altered werewolf voice was a welcome sound as he bellowed from the distance, "Snow! Down boy!"

The beautiful white wolf ceased his snarling, but he didn't move an inch.

No longer feeling threatened, I turned in the direction that the command came from just in time to see Noah leap through the air toward us. His strong legs had managed to catapult him over yards of ground with one single bound. I found it incredibly impressive.

"Lisa, is that you?" he asked as he cautiously approached Snow and me. His voice had a tone to it that I couldn't decipher. Was it anger or sadness when he said, "It smells like you. You've shifted to full wolf form."

I wanted to say something, but could only make canine sounds.

When he moved a bit closer, my heightened sensed took in the familiar smell of his body. The combination of his human

283

and werewolf pheromones was all the more appealing to me. I could feel my body reacting with a type of animal desire.

Memories of laying in his arms while I listened to the beat of his heart as he slept, mixed with the passion of our love making, filled my head. I felt such an overwhelming sense of loss and sadness that my eyes flooded with tears to the point that they slid down my snout.

Compassion radiated from his words as he moved forward and cupped my snout in his strong, werewolf hands. "It is you," he said. "I'm so very sorry. I should never have let you go. Now, look what happened. You didn't want this. I know that you didn't. I should have kept you safe."

I gave a meek sounding canine whimper as I reveled in his touch.

"Let's get you to the cabin," he said in a soft tone. "We can wait out the moon together."

Just then, the sound of Caleb and his pack permeated the trees. Noah snarled his disapproval.

"Snow," he commanded, "Stand steady."

Out of the darkness appeared Caleb's pack. Forming a circle, they slowly closed in around us until their faces could be easily seen in the tree filtered moonlight.

"Stand aside," Caleb bellowed as he

broke through the circle to position himself between Noah and me. "This is my intended mate. Back away."

Noah looked at me with eyes that expressed both surprise and sadness.

Even though he knew that I couldn't reply, he softly asked, "Is this true?"

"It is, but it is not!" bellowed Oscar's altered voice as he bounded into the center of the circle in his fully impressive werewolf form. "I introduced Lisa to Caleb with the intention of him taking her as a mate, but I do not know if she agreed. She's been held captive these past weeks and we've been forbidden to get near her. Kenzie tried every day."

"So, that's where she disappeared to," Noah said with a hint of *ahhh ha* in his voice.

"She asked us not to tell you because she was angry with you," Oscar continued.

Noah looked at the ground.

"I made a mistake that I'll regret forever," he said. "I let Danica and my pack influence my stupidity." Looking at me, he said with sincerity, "It was never about Danica. I never loved or wanted to mate with her. It's you, Lisa. It's all you. It doesn't matter about your genetics. The pack will have to get past that because I've fallen in love with you. The last few days of missing you and not knowing where to reach you have ripped at my heart. Please don't mate with him until you've given me a chance."

"I have it on good authority that you're the one she wants to mate with," bellowed Kenzie from off in the darkness.

Oscar and Noah simultaneously sucked in air. I could feel their panic, as I felt it too. What on earth was Kenzie thinking? We were surrounded by a pack of werewolves who were about to fight over possession of me. To top it off, they had no love for humans. It didn't matter that she was with Oscar. Oscar was of the opposing pack. All that bit of information did was to give them even greater cause to tear her to pieces.

His concern for her safety was clear as Oscar shouted, "What are you doing here? Leave now!"

In a deliberate act of defiance, Kenzie boldly marched into the center of the circle to stand next to me.

Looking directly at Caleb, she hissed, "You have your nerve, Caleb Smythe. We left our girl with you in good faith
and what did you do? You're no better than the werewolf scum we were trying to protect her from."

Caleb gave a wry smirk as he looked at my friend with disdain.

"Your opinion of me matters not," he

said. "You're a human with no understanding of our ways. Lisa and I have already coupled. She's mine. All we lack is the mating ritual. Kindly step aside and I will take care of that fact."

"You'll do no such thing," Kenzie hissed. "If coupling lays claim, then Noah has first dibs! I happen to know that she lay with him before she even met you."

"That's a lie!" Danica bellowed from within the crowd.

"It most certainly is not," Kenzie said, "and I'll wager she wasn't forced by Noah. Since she's been a prisoner of yours, Caleb, I'm assuming that she was also not a willing partner in bed."

"It wasn't rape," he defensively said.

"There are many forms of rape," she replied with disdain.

Danica lept from the circle of werewolves and pushed Kenzie to the ground.

"How dare you speak to him like that?" she snarled. "You, a mere human." Turning to Oscar, she said with a venomous tone, "You're the scum for pairing up with such a worthless creature. Now you can kiss your human goodbye."

Kenzie looked directly at her attacker as she said with a firm and confident tone, "You don't frighten me, Danica. None of you do."

"That's your mistake," Danica snarled.

I never considered myself to be a hero or even all that brave, but the fear I felt for Kenzie's wellbeing turned into rage when I saw Danica raise her claw like hand. I could not only see that she intended to strike the life from my closest friend with one swift swipe, but my psyche picked up on Danica's thoughts. Suddenly, something came over me. Without concern for myself or what the outcome might be, I snarled with fury as I pounced on the hateful she-wolf.

A loud thud filled my ears as she flew off Kenzie and landed on the ground. Without a moment's hesitation, my strong teeth were locked in a vice grip on her thick, hairy throat. I could taste her werewolf blood as she screamed for someone to help her.

Expecting to be torn from my prey at any moment, I defiantly locked my jaw into place. There was no way I was going to allow this bitch to kill my friend. The hate that I felt for her in human form was intensified tenfold now that I was in wolf form.

I was aware of Snow circling us as he warned the other werewolves to back off. It was then that I realized that a wolf in full form was a formidable opponent for a werewolf. This explained why Caleb announced that he'd need help to subdue me enough to mate with me. It also made the relationship between Snow and Noah all the more impressive.

As a wolf, my peripheral vision was excellent. While I placed my full weight on Danica's torso and continued to clamp down on her throat, I could see that Noah and Caleb had entered into battle. Was it over mating with me? Or was it a conflict about what I was doing to Caleb's cousin? I'd been so engrossed in my attack on Danica that I missed their exchange of words so I couldn't be sure.

Oscar was quick to take advantage of the chaos and scoop Kenzie up and away. I could hear her loud protests about not being afraid of werewolves and wanting to protect me as her voice faded into the distance. I made a mental note to thank her for her loyalty before I chastised her for her stupidity once I was human again.

43

I could feel the life force slowly ebbing from Danica. The human part of my mind reasoned that, with Kenzie out of danger, the right thing to do would have been to release her, but the wolf in me refused to let go. The urge to finished the job and tear her throat out was so intense that I trembled from the effort to resist it.

The shouts of the crowd around me as they rooted for their pack leader to take Noah down and finish him off only served to drive my animal instinct to kill even further. I'm not sure if I'd have resisted much longer had Oscar not returned with Noah's pack.

With the numbers on a more equal basis, Caleb's pack quieted down. I took note of this fact. Apparently, not only was Noah a strong leader, but his pack was ready to fiercely defend him if the need arose.

From what I could see, they need do nothing. Although Caleb managed to get in a few good punches, bites, and throw downs,

Noah was steadily overtaking him.

When Noah pinned Caleb beneath him with such force that I felt a gust of wind on my face, it was clear that Caleb's pack either didn't feel up to the task or weren't loyal enough to bother to step in and give him the aide that he needed. Little by little, they dwindled away until only a handful remained to see their leader's throat torn out by the love of my life.

Encouraged by the fact that Noah had killed Caleb, I sank my teeth deeper into Danica's flesh. To my disappointment, Noah's strong hand gently nudged my snout until I'd released her neck.

"There's no need to kill her, my love," he said in a soft tone. "She was simply defending her pack master. It was not only expected of her, but she was the only one loyal enough to do it. She should be rewarded for her bravery, not killed for it." Shaking his head, he looked at the few remaining members of Caleb's pack and said, "Your pack master is dead. It's good that he didn't see what a sorry lot you are before he died. Take him home and give him a proper send off." He focused his eyes on Danica as he continued with, "I don't recommend that any of you enter our territory again." He waited for them to retrieve Caleb's body and disappear into the woods before resting his hand on my head and addressing his pack members. "This is Lisa. She is a mutt, but she is also the love of my life. I intend to mate with her. If any of you disapprove, you are free to leave the pack. Or, if you prefer, I will step down from pack master."

There was a low grumbling amongst them before a mere few walked away. I watched in awe as the remaining members knelt down and bowed their heads. I assumed that this meant that they were fine with his announcement. Or, at least, they had no intension of disrupting the dynamics of the pack because of it.

"Let's go back to the cabin now," he said to me as he scratched between my ears. Then, with a low chuckle, he added, "You make a beautiful wolf, by the way."

I flashed my teeth and snipped in response before racing off to the cabin. Noah was quick to catch up with me. For someone with only two legs, he managed to keep pace with my four legs just fine.

Exhausted from the ordeal of the day and the night, I curled up in front of the fireplace next to Snow and fell into a deep sleep. When I awoke, I was human and quite naked.

Sitting up, I looked around the room. With the exception of my faithful white wolf, it was empty.

Somehow, my red cape had been retrieved

and was now covering my nakedness. The clothes that I'd worn to meet Caleb were neatly folded on one of the sofa cushions. I wasn't sure, but I suspected it was Noah's doing.

Wrapping the cape around me, I stood up and made my way to his bedroom.

He looked irresistibly handsome as he lay in deep slumber. The covers that shielded his nakedness from prying eyes gave a clear outline of his powerful physique. Even in human form, he was a sight to behold.

I let the cape fall to the floor as I slid beneath the covers alongside him. The heat of his body felt comforting and inviting as he instinctively wrapped me into his arms and pulled me close. I wanted nothing more than to make love to him right then, but I could see that he was exhausted. Not only that, but he'd suffered a good beating from Caleb before he managed to best him. It would be cruel of me not to give him time to heal.

I smiled with lustful anticipation as I remembered how quickly he would heal. In the matter of just a few hours, he'd be as good as new.

Closing my eyes, I snuggled into him. The rhythmic beating of his heart lured me toward a secure and confident sleep.

I was almost lost in slumber when I heard him say in a low, voice that still echoed a hint of his werewolf self, "Oscar says that you are of royal blood and not a mutt. He says that you are of the McKean pack. Is this true?"

Remembering my great, great, great, great grandfather's fears about how Noah might take the news that I was a McKean, I swallowed hard while I slowly nodded.

"Does it change things?" I asked. "I know your pack opposed their decision to bind our werewolfism."

"That was a long time ago," he said. "I hold no animosity. I simply wish that you had told me earlier. It would have prevented a lot of problems."

"I didn't know until recently," I confessed. Then, with a mischievous giggle, I snuggled into his chest and said, "Besides, it was nice to hear you announce your love for me even though you thought I was a mutt." When he gave me a light squeeze, I added, "Do you want to know what was even better to hear?"

He kissed the top of my head and said, "Sure."

"It was when you admitted that you'd been stupid."

I rolled with laughter as he playfully growled before kissing me long and hard.

A Sneak Peek at Vickie: Doctor by day. Zombie Hunter by night

Eileen Sheehan

"Why should I fear death? If I am, death is not. If death is, I am not. Why should I fear that which cannot exist when I do?"
—Epicurus

ONE

I can't remember a time when I wasn't trying to help heal someone or something. As a little girl on my family's dairy farm, I made it my mission to help my father with the care of the animals. Such was my dedication that when I found a baby bird that fell out of its nest, I took great pains to nurse it to health and see that it was able to care for itself before I set it free.

Originally, I was determined to heal others the old-fashioned way, with herbs and energy work. I'd read plenty of how-to books on the subject and even taken a few online courses. When I left the farm as soon as I graduated high school and moved to find my way in the nearby city of Winchester, Virginia. I even went as far as to open my own holistic practice.

It was when I attended a six-week course through the local college's community education program on herbal remedies that I decided that it was okay to integrate herbal and energy healing with modern medicine. I really didn't need the course. I'd poured myself into that world for so many years that there was very little in the line of herbal remedies or reiki energy work left for me to learn. I just enjoyed taking the classes and mixing with likeminded people who got a kick out of exchanging herbal remedy recipes and reiki sessions.

Dr. Peter Thomason was the instructor of this class. I didn't know for sure, but I guessed him to be in his early thirties. He was not only full of excitement for life, but I found him incredibly handsome and charismatic. It was more than his looks; which, in themselves, were enough to mesmerize any healthy, red-blooded female. I couldn't imagine anyone being able to resist his royal blue eyes that were made to look even bluer by the thick black lashes that framed them and his sun-bronzed skin as a background. He had a full head of shoulder length hair that was almost ebony black with hints of sunlight running through it. They were more prominent in the out of doors than under the florescent lights of the classroom. He wore his generous head of hair pulled back in an old-fashioned queue for most of the classes, but there were a few times when he simply let it fall wildly about. When he did, it framed his high cheek bones and square jaw in such a way as to make me wish it was my arms wrapped so possessively around such beauty instead of that hair. I would sit in the back of the room and revel in the sight of the lean, muscular physique that I was sure existed beneath his baggy linen shirt and pants.

On the few occasions when I was near enough, the pheromones he emitted practically drove me to the point that I needed to either leave the room or jump his bones; which was saying a lot because I was still a virgin. Since we were in a classroom with other students- and, even if we were alone, I was too inexperienced to know how to lure him into taking me right there on his desk- I opted to leave the room. I'd visit the ladies room for a splash of cool water on my face and a good one-on-one scolding between me and my reflection in the mirror.

He'd recently arrived from a tour with Doctors Without Borders in Africa, which was where he got that memorable tan. More than once, he'd share a tale or two of what it was like for him to treat those in need with both herbs and modern medicine. It was through his stories that I concluded that both had their place, and both had their value. It soon became clear to me that by combining the two, I'd be able to heal a lot more efficiently and effectively. By the time the six-week course was over, I was looking at colleges to attend for my medical degree.

Sadly, Dr. Thomason was scheduled to

go on yet another tour with Doctors Without Borders shortly after the course ended, but I managed to convince him to have coffee with me to discuss my plans to go to medical school before we said our good-byes. Admittedly, I would have preferred our conversation between the sheets after a ridiculously long marathon of love making instead of at Starbucks while drinking a latte and eating a cheese Danish, but no matter. The meeting with the oh so handsome Dr. Peter Thomason, die-hard good Samaritan, was so intense and profound that it solidified my determination to become a medical doctor.

That was twelve years ago.

With my residency behind me, and a medical license finally in my grasp, life became a whirlwind of busy and full, but there were still times when I had a few moments of quiet to reflect on things that a vision of the handsome Dr. Peter Thomason popped into my mind and I wondered what good deeds he was doing and what third world was he doing them in.

As for what was happening with me in my world... I'd accepted a
position as the town physician in a small community, called Wolf Junction, in
the hills of West Virginia, not far from Mechanicsville. It wasn't that I didn't have opportunities to join the staff at a few

prestigious hospitals. I'd even been offered a position at a couple of holistic clinics that specialized in using both traditional and alternative medicine when dealing with illnesses such as cancer. I was seriously considering one particular clinic in Phoenix when I learned of the position as town doctor in Wolf Junction. At first, I paid it little mind. After all, I may have been a newly licensed physician, but, not only was I top in my class, I was also highly knowledgeable in herbal and energy medicine. The idea of the freedom being a town doctor would offer over that of a clinic with its hierarchy and rules was alluring. I'd done my residency in a big city hospital with its mega rules, regulations, and jealous competitiveness amongst peers. Being able to work on my own and call the shots was definitely appealing. When I read the report on the recent outbreak of death by mysterious causes, I was sold. The idea of being the physician to discover the illness that was killing a goodly number of Wolf Junction residents when others were stumped was far too alluring. I just had to accept the offer. Besides, it would also provide me the freedom I so valued when it came to integrating alternative and traditional medicine. The depths of the Blue Ridge Mountains weren't exactly third world, but society in small towns tended to be less progressive than most of the country. It was as close to third world as I was going to get.

So, with my medical degree and license proudly in hand, I packed my bags and headed off to Wolf Junction and my new life as Dr. Vickie Anderson, the town physician.

Little did I know what I was getting myself in for.

TWO

Wolf Junction may not have been as advanced both socially and economically as the rest of the country, but it was filled with history. To me, this made up for a lot.

The home I'd rented was an enormous Victorian style house with a gorgeous wrap around porch. It was far too large for one person, but it had a two-room office set up with a space to act as the waiting room and its own entrance. I was of the frame of mind that having my office under the same roof where I lived would reduce my overhead. After all, I'd built up a considerable amount of debt putting myself through school. Fortunately, my holistic care skills paid for most of my living expenses during my years of education, but there was still the loan for the actual cost of schooling looming over me. As luck would have it, the place came partially furnished. So, I lived in a one-hundred plus year old house that was the size of a mini-hotel with enough décor in it to make it look occupied. Had the place not come with furnishings enough to soften the interior of the grand house, my bank account would have allowed me to select a room or two to furnish while leaving the rest to the ghosts whose voices echoed off the walls some nights.

I'm not being dramatic when I say the walls echoed voices. It was my own fault for going through a realtor and renting the place from the recommendation of the realtor and the photos I saw on the website. Had I inspected it in person, I would have found the set up in the basement for the mortician to embalm and prepare the bodies to be laid out upstairs in the viewing rooms.

For some reason unbeknownst to me, the realtor left the fact that I was renting a former funeral home out of all communications. Since there was no law stating that its former use needed to be divulged, there was nothing I could do about it but remind myself that I was a woman of science and medicine. The residue of death didn't, shouldn't, and wouldn't bother me.

For a small community, the town of Wolf Junction managed to keep two funeral homes in business right up until Jack Crowley, the mortician who owned my home, died a quiet and peaceful death three years earlier. Running a funeral home had been a Crowley family tradition right up until Jack's death ended it. Jack's wife pre-deceased him by ten years. Sadly, they were childless and not one of his relatives felt obliged to pick up where he left off. The house was one of the few things left in the estate that the relatives hung on to. Whether it was for sentimental reasons, since it was a Crowley who'd built it, or if it was for investment purposes, I couldn't say. They tried to find another funeral director to take the place over, but, after three years of no interest, they put it with a realtor to rent and, well, you know the rest.

Business was slow at first. Some of the townspeople were leery about patronizing a doctor who lived in and worked out of a funeral home, while others worried about the fact that I was so young. It didn't help that the doctor I replaced -who had died of old age in his sleep- treated the townsfolk for over sixty years. His shoes were tough ones to fill.

What went to my advantage was my knowledge of alternative remedies. I quickly discovered that the locals were more trusting of things that came from mother nature than they were with what came from the pharmacist at the neighborhood drug store. So, I started out peddling the holistic side of my services and slowly slipped the medical into the mix.

By the end of the third month, things looked like they just might work out for me.

Although there was still room for plenty more, I had enough patients to fill up at least three days out of the week; although I spread them out throughout the five as best I could. I used my free time to explore the area, as well as my enormous house.

Wolf Junction was a small town amidst other small towns that were nestled in the hills of the Blue Ridge Mountains. I was delighted to discover the myriad of antique shops these towns possessed. History abounded.

It was in one of these quaint shops that I struck up a conversation with the woman behind the sales counter. She was old enough to qualify as an antique herself, but she had the feistiness of a young woman in her persona. Her name was Megan Hastings and I found her delightful.

Megan was a walking encyclopedia of just about any topic that came up, or so it seemed. She also had a great head on her shoulders when it came to pragmatic subjects; such as the fact that I was rambling around in that grand house when I could have the company of a boarder or two.

What a great idea!

As luck would have it, Megan even knew of a few professionals who would appreciate living arrangements like that. One was a social worker who traveled through the area regularly checking on her cases. Megan was sure that she would appreciate having a steady place to stay where she could keep a few belongings.

The other would probably be a more temporary situation. He was a novelist who believed he wrote best if he planted himself in the geographical area that he was placing his characters in and exposed himself to the environments or situations that were similar to what he created in his story lines. It was her understanding that he planned on staying for at least a year. He'd visited Megan's shop and struck up a conversation with her enough for her to feel confident in recommending him as a boarder. She had no doubt he'd be thrilled to leave the boarding house he spoke so poorly about.

It took less than two weeks to interview these two potential boarders, check their references, and set them up in one of the many bedrooms that my house had. In fact, a few of the rooms had Jack and Jill bathrooms so I was able to rent out the two rooms to create a little private living space as well for each of them. Megan was not only a feisty old gal with a winning personality, she was a genius.

I took the rent from the boarders and designated it to help pay off my innumerable debts from school. This allowed me to re-invest money that I earned from my health care practice back into it.

Eileen Sheehan

Life was good.

THREE

Angela McGraw was a few years older than me, but not by much. We looked to be about the same size too, but that's where the similarities ended. Where my hair was sleek and dark, and my skin fair and unblemished, she sported a coppery head of wiry curls and flesh so peppered with freckles that it was impossible to count them. As my eyes traced them to the collar of her pale blue cotton blouse, I had to fight the urge to ask if they continued onto her back and chest. I guessed they did, but that was just a guess. I envied her those striking green eyes. Mine were such a common brown. I noticed that they resembled rich emerald when she spoke passionately on a subject; which was often.

She'd been, working as the county's traveling social worker for five years. It was easy to tell that she loved her job by the way she lost herself into conversing about it whenever the opportunity arose.

She was less outgoing and generous

with words and information when it came to discussing herself and her family. The background checks I'd done showed me that she'd lost her parents when she was in her early teens and was taken in by her aunt and uncle on her mother's side. Although she didn't say, I got the impression that she wasn't very fond of them and was eager to leave the nest as soon as she came of age. Her brother, Michael, was two years older than her. He died while fighting in Iraq. Her pain over losing him echoed
in her words as she told the tale.

She was a vegetarian and an animal activist with a special affinity for cats. She didn't own a pet for the simple reason that she was traveling too much and couldn't take it with her, but it was something she longed to have. Because it's my philosophy that people should think before they speak, I didn't offer to let her have a cat. I needed to see how well she worked out as a boarder first. I also wanted to see how much she'd be home to take care of it.

Evan Ottenburg was the writer. Information on him was a bit harder to acquire, but I managed to get enough to feel comfortable about renting to him. He was a clean cut, nice looking guy who was in his mid-thirties. Unlike Angela, his features didn't make him stand out as soon as he entered a room. He blended with the crowd in a way that allowed him the anonymity I assumed he sought when people watching and coming up with ideas for his stories.

It didn't hurt that he'd already met Angela in passing while visiting Megan's shop and they spoke of each other in a way that made me believe them to be compatible. Just to make sure, I held a small dinner party and invited them, along with Megan, the sheriff, Max Orwell, and the owner of the town's weekly paper, Joslin Camp.

As I'd expected, Evan and Joslin took an instant liking to each other. It was by listening to their conversation that I learned that Evan started his writing career as a journalist for the New York Post. He eventually grew tired of the rat race and tried his hand at writing fiction. His talent as a word sleuth, combined with his connections in the media world, gave him the foundation to help get the publicity he needed for his first novel to become a best seller. He wrote under a pseudo-name, but I learned that was quite common. A lot of writers did this for a variety of reasons, mainly the anonymity factor.

I chuckled when I saw Angela's reaction to Max when he stepped onto my front porch and offered me a bottle of wine as his contribution to the evening. I'd had the same reaction when I first met him. Who wouldn't? He stood an easy inch or two over six feet tall with shoulders that resembled those of a football player. His broad chest tapered down to narrow hips and a tight butt. His pants didn't hug his thighs, but I could tell that they were well-formed and muscular. I expected him to tell me that he was a body builder, but it was far from the truth. He got his powerful physique from the hard labor that was required of successful farmers and he kept it by keeping busy in the out of doors doing things like hunting, camping, and hiking. He was also known to pitch in during haying season should a farmer find himself shorthanded, which was often. His thick, sandy blonde hair was just long enough to cover the top of his ears. It fell across his forehead in a way that drew attention to his sky-blue eyes.

Had I been looking for a boyfriend, I would have definitely set my sights on Max. As it was, I was far too focused on getting my career off the ground to want to spare the time I felt would be necessary to maintain a relationship with a man that was anything more than casual friendship.

This had been my thought process since I'd graduated high school.

Believe it or not, I went on exactly two dates while in college; both of which turned out disastrous. I was of the frame of mind that dinner and a movie warranted a thank you and a nice evening kiss while my dates felt it deserved a wild bout in bed. Since I was still a virgin and found neither of them hot enough to tempt me to change that status at the time, I sent them packing. They didn't call for a second date and I was just as happy. I knew that when the time was right, I'd settle down with a man. Now just wasn't the time. Since I'd always been fine with my own company, I wasn't worried.

Dinner proved not only entertaining, but it seeded the beginning of several friendships. Once again, I praised Megan for her genius. I couldn't imagine how different my life would have been had I never walked into her antique shop.

Eileen Sheehan

About the Author

Eileen Sheehan primarily writes hot, steamy romances (mostly New Adult) with a sexy male and strong female. A few are steamier than others (see their description). The majority of her novels are paranormal, but some are novels about normal people in love (contemporary or historical with the author name of Ailene Frances). ALL of her stories have a bit of naughtiness, some excitement, a few thrills, and maybe a touch of mystery mixed in with sometimes hot, sometimes sweet lovin'. She strives to write a novel length that will allow the busy woman to be able to sit down in an evening or two and be taken on a romantic journey without having a week go by before she gets to the end of the story. Most of her novels take the average reader five to six hours to read.

An incurable romantic, she has a love affair with at least one of her characters... one book at a time. She hopes the same thing happens to you.

***

Eileen Sheehan started out as a freelance writer for periodical magazines and newspapers. From there, she tried her hand at writing screenplays. Her screenplay, "When East Meets West" was a finalist in the

2001 Independent International Film and Video Festival at Madison Square Gardens, NYC. Finally finding her niche, she lets her imagination loose with new adult/paranormal romance/thrillers (some are steamy and some are tame) with the author name of Eileen Sheehan. She creates steamy historical and contemporary romances with the author name of Ailene Frances. Since she enjoys a bit of adrenaline releasing now and then, she writes mystery/thrillers with the author name of Eileen F. Sheehan. Seeing how far out of the box she could stretch, she crafted an alternative romance with the author name of E. F. Sheehan and has a few self-help books under her work name of Lena Sheehan.

Eileen Sheehan

Other Books by Eileen Sheehan

[Most are available in eBook, paperback & audio format]

[GENRE: PARANORMAL
ROMANCE/THRILLERS]
THE VAMPIRE, THE HANDLER, AND ME
FOR LOVE OF A VAMPIRE
THE PRINCESS AND THE VAMPIRE KING
(Also in audio)
A VAMPIRE'S LOVE (also in audio)
EMERGENCE
DRAGON LOVE
DREAM LOVE
GHOST LOVE
SISTERS
OF WOLVES AND MEN

Dark Escape Duo
DARK ESCAPE (Book 1)
THE SEARCH FOR THE CRYSTAL KEY
(Book 2)

Tugurlan Chronicles

Of Wolves and Men
VAMPIRE INIQUITY (Book 1)
THE CURE (Book 2)
VAMPIRES AND WEREWOLVES (Book 3)

Vampire Witch Trilogy
VAMPIRE WITCH (Book 1)
VAMPIRE QUEEN (Book 2)
KINGS & QUEENS (Book 3)

Shadow Love Duo
SHADOW LOVE: BOOK ONE
SHADOW LOVE: BOOK TWO

a Wolf Affair Trilogy
a WOLF AFFAIR (Book 1)
WOLF MOUNTAIN (Book 2)
MISSY'S CHOICE (Book 3)

The Adventures of Vickie Anderson
VICKIE: Doctor by day. Zombie hunter by
night (Book 1)
VICKIE: Doctor by day. Werewolf hunter by
night (Book 2)

Eileen Sheehan

The Adventures of Vickie Anderson Cont.

VICKIE: Doctor by day. Ghost hunter by
night (Book 3)

VICKIE: Doctor by day. Vampire medic by
night (Book 4)

Kendra's Journey

WHERE ZOMBIES WALK (Book 1)

THE REGIME (Book 2)

CENTER LAND (Book 3)

ZOMBIES AND ALIENS (Book 4)

The Esmerelda Sleuth Series

THE OTHER SIDE OF THE MIRROR (Book 1)

THE MAGIC BOX (Book 2)

BEYOND THE PORTAL (Book 3)

THE JOURNAL (Book 4)

****

BOOKS BY AILENE FRANCES

[GENRE: ROMANCE]

Of Wolves and Men

BOOKS BY AILENE FRANCES CONT.

LOVE MISUNDERSTOOD

(Historical Georgian Era Romance)

PAPER WIDOW

(Historical Western Romance)

LOVE AT WOLF CREEK

(Historical Western Romance)

FOR LOVE OR MONEY

(Contemporary Mid-Western Romance)

****

BOOKS BY E. F. SHEEHAN

[GENRE: ALTERNATIVE ROMANCE/DRAMA]

TOAST WITH JELLY

A Tragedy of a Lesbian Confused

****

BOOKS BY LENA SHEEHAN

[GENRE: SELF-HELP]

HUMAN, HELP THYSELF

Natural Solutions for Stress of Body, Mind & Spirit

BASIC HYPNOSIS

ALL ABOUT REIKI